A
Harlequin
Romance

OTHER
Harlequin Romances

by REBECCA STRATTON

Many of these titles are available at your local bookseller,
or through the Harlequin Reader Service.

For a free catalogue listing all available Harlequin Romances,
send your name and address to:

HARLEQUIN READER SERVICE,
M.P.O. Box 707, Niagara Falls, N.Y. 14302
Canadian address: Stratford, Ontario, Canada N5A 6W4

or use order coupon at back of books.

CHATEAU D'ARMOR

by

REBECCA STRATTON

Harlequin Books

TORONTO • LONDON • NEW YORK • AMSTERDAM • SYDNEY • WINNIPEG

Original hardcover edition published in 1976
by Mills & Boon Limited

ISBN 0-373-02018-X

Harlequin edition published November 1976

Printed in U.S.A.

CHAPTER ONE

Jesamine Arden, journalist at large, sounded very grand, but Jesamine felt she had earned the title, for this was her fourth trip to Europe in six months, though her first to France. Being freelance had its advantages, she thought, although it meant that she was very much on her own when anything went wrong with the planned schedule – as now.

James Terril had come with her as far as Nantes, but there he had been stricken with a particularly malevolent virus and transported hurriedly to the nearest hospital. James was to have taken the pictures illustrating the article she was to write, but as she watched him go off in the ambulance she had decided to take his whispered advice and go on alone. The photographs could be taken later, when he recovered sufficiently to follow her. In the meantime she could carry on to Grosvallée and get to know her subject.

The idea of linking families in England with their ancestral roots in the various Common Market countries had been her own, and Jesamine was rather proud of it. *Woman's Life*, for whom she had worked before, had taken up the idea enthusiastically and she had been given a more or less free hand, as long as she produced a series of eight articles within a specified time.

The fact that she was well ahead with her schedule was thanks largely to the fact that she was a willing traveller and, after choosing the families she wanted in England, she dashed around Europe tracking down their Common Market roots with a zest that brought co-operation from the most unlikely quarters. She had left France until last for her own specific reasons, and she faced this trip with even more than her usual excitement.

The coincidence of her own family being connected to the d'Armor family in the Loire valley area of France had only been revealed when she spoke about the project to her maternal grandfather, and it added spice to the whole scheme to think that she was closely involved herself.

Jesamine had often wished that she could have seen more of her grandfather during her childhood, but his career as a sea captain had made that impossible, since he was so often away, though she had always been fond of him. A big, weathered man, he had the traditional seaman's gift for telling a story, and she had listened with interest and excitement when he related his family's history, a history she had been unaware of, except as a vague fact in the background, until now. Leaving her own story until last had been deliberate, for it gave her more time to spend on the project and still meet her scheduled limit.

She had listened raptly while her grandfather told her about a certain Charles Louis Vernais, Comte d'Armor, who fled from France in the year 1793, following the execution of King Louis XVI. From her grandfather she learned that the line descended directly through his side of the family via Louise Sutton, an English squire's daughter who had taken the fancy of the escaping French nobleman.

The gallant Comte, however, had not lingered long enough to marry the lady, but her son, who was also called Charles, had eventually married respectably and founded the family from which descended Jesamine's own mother. She had frankly admitted to one or two qualms when she first wrote to the present head of the d'Armor family and it came to mentioning her own nebulous connection with them, but his reply had been very gracious and helpful.

Not only had he offered her every assistance in her task, but added the hope that she would honour them by staying at the Château d'Armor during her sojourn in France, however long it might be – the invitation to include her companion, James Terril, as well.

It was a pity about James, she thought, but there was little she could do to help him even if she stayed in Nantes until he was well again, and she could not still the fluttering sense of excitement she felt as she neared her destination. Driving through the lovely Breton countryside she could think of little else but the coming meeting with the family d'Armor.

It was incredibly exciting to think that the people she was on her way to see were linked with her own family by ties that went back almost two hundred years, and the feeling got stronger the nearer she got to Grosvallée and the Château d'Armor.

The hire car she was driving had been meant to take both her and James to the château, but she had only a few minor qualms about leaving him to drive on alone, for she felt that this journey was something very special. There was an historically romantic link here that she felt she wanted to discover alone – James could come into the matter later when she had made the first approach.

She had researched the project with her usual thoroughness before she left home, but the information available on their personal lives had proved sparse, although their reputation as wine producers was in no doubt at all. They were among the best known in the area, and in the Loire valley that was quite a reputation to have.

She had managed to learn one or two facts about the family members, however, enough to give her some idea of their characters, she thought, and she was confident she could manage the interview as successfully as she had the others in the series. Her main task would be to establish the actual connection between her own family and the d'Armors and if possible make friends with them so that they saw her as a distant link in their own history and not simply as a journalist after a story.

The letter she had received from Monsieur François d'Armor suggested that it would be possible to get to know them quite well, for he sounded quite charming and willing to help in any way he could. Once that certain rapport was established she could then go on to write a potted history of the two families, to be illustrated by the photographs James would take later of the château and its surroundings.

The car was handling well, and she had somehow managed to remember to drive on the right-hand side of the road, even while she was preoccupied with admiring the countryside. It reminded her rather of parts of Wales she had visited, and she recalled that she had once read somewhere that Brittany and Wales had quite a lot in common, both historically and linguistically.

Both could claim to have been ancient kingdoms in their own right, much fought over and hardly subdued, and their language and cultures were very similar. Both people were still very Celtic in character too, being fiercely nationalistic and proud of their traditions. It was a land of beautiful forests and moors, of clear bright streams and lovely valleys. It was, Jesamine decided on first acquaintance, well worth the visit even had she had nothing else in mind but sightseeing.

She was now in the Loire valley region and the first glimpse of vineyards gave her a tingling thrill, for it meant she could not have so much further to go. The d'Armor vineyards were famous and produced the grapes for one of the very fine wines for which the area was justly famed. Everything was new, delightful and exciting, and she felt

8

no more than a small twinge of guilt for having left James behind.

She was so entranced by the view that she almost missed seeing a sign erected at the turn of a sudden and rather sharp bend and indicating the way to Grosvallée. It was because she so nearly missed her turning that she spun the wheel round hard to cope with the sharp curve and consequently took the corner very wide.

She hung on grimly when she realised that she had misjudged badly and prayed there was nothing coming from the other direction. The hire car veered round, its tyres shrieking on the rough surface, and came jerkily to a standstill on the wrong side of the road and hair-raisingly close to the bonnet of a big, dark Mercedes that braked to a halt, though not quite soon enough to avoid hitting her.

Jesamine sat still behind the wheel for a second, her heart thudding heavily, not only in alarm at the near-accident, but because she was so obviously in the wrong, and the driver of the Mercedes was already out of his seat and frowning darkly at the front of his car. Another couple of strides and he was facing Jesamine as she stepped out to meet him, gazing anxiously at the two cars now apparently bound together inextricably by their bumpers.

The man was tall, too tall for her to feel at ease, for he towered over her, and he had ice-grey eyes that glittered angrily as he spoke to her in French, apparently under the impression she was a compatriot. "*Qu'avez-vous, mademoiselle?*" he demanded. "*Etes-vous insensée?*"

Jesamine was pale and she felt more than a little shaky, though it seemed not to concern him in the least. A steep drop into the vine-covered valley yawned only inches from the front wheels of their vehicles, and she was too shaken by the thought of what might have happened to even resent his abuse. Instead she swallowed hard and shook her head.

"I – I don't speak French," she told him, and the watching eyes narrowed slightly, she thought, although she had paid little heed to his appearance so far.

"You are English, *mademoiselle*?" he asked, and she nodded. "So!" He shrugged resignedly, as if that explained it all. "You drive on the wrong side of the road!"

"But I *wasn't!*" Jesamine denied hastily. She noted the way he glanced at the hired car, bumper to bumper with his and on the wrong side of the road, and she shook her head. "I almost missed the sign to Grosvallée," she explained. "I might have taken the corner a little wide."

"As you say, *mademoiselle*!" He indicated the locked bumpers and frowned. "It will not be easy to disengage," he guessed, "and I have an appointment in half an hour!"

"I'm sorry!" She looked on helplessly. It was useless for her to suggest anything, for she had no mechanical knowledge at all, and always had to depend on someone else to solve problems like this. "If I could help," she ventured, convinced he would refuse, but to her dismay he nodded.

"Take one side of the *pare-choc*," he told her, and frowned again when she looked mystified. "The bumper, *mademoiselle*! We can lift my car free!"

He walked around to the other side, seeming to stand dangerously close to that long drop into the valley, and put his hands on the bumper of the car. Being the bigger vehicle it was on top, but to Jesamine it suggested an incredible feat of strength to move it, and she blinked in dismay at being expected to help.

"Can we do it?" she asked, looking doubtfully at the big car, and the man gave her a pitying look.

He was already rocking the vehicle and heaving on the metal bumper with both hands. "*We* can, *mademoiselle*," he informed her tersely. "Alone I think I may not! Lend me your assistance, *s'il vous plaît*, I have to be on my way!"

There was nothing for it but to do as he said, and Jesamine moved round, laying hold of it as he did, amazed to find that it actually worked and the two cars parted. Even so, with her inexpertness, she bruised the fingers of one hand when they eventually achieved their object. The cry she gave was completely ignored, however, indeed she doubted if he even noticed it, and she stood with her bruised knuckles pressed to her mouth, looking at him reproachfully.

He examined his own vehicle for damage, but omitted to do as much for hers, then he turned and looked at her, and she really saw him for the first time. He was not as she would have described a typical Frenchman, although she was in some doubt if there was such a thing. Somehow she thought of them as dark, typically Gallic, but this man was quite fair, with thick straight hair, and those steely grey eyes that now regarded her with almost embarrassing interest.

He was not good-looking, rather too strong and rugged for that, with craggy features that were well tanned by sun and weather as if he spent most of his time out of doors, although that gleaming dark car scarcely suggested a farm-worker and neither did his manner. He was self-assured to the point of being arrogant, and he was looking at her now as if she was some kind of inferior being, albeit an attractive one.

Jesamine was not unused to men showing an interest in her, for she had her share of good looks. Petite in build with a slim rounded figure and a small oval face; she had long black hair and blue eyes that were fringed with dark lashes and large as a child's. She never failed to attract masculine attention, but there was something quite blatantly speculative about this man's gaze that caused her a twinge of uneasiness, and she condemned herself for a fool for standing there talking to him on an apparently deserted road.

She was no more easy when he eased his firm, straight mouth into a faintly ironic smile suddenly. "I hope, *mademoiselle,* that you are now aware of the dangers of driving on the wrong side of the road!" Briefly he inclined his head in a curtly formal bow. "I trust you will achieve the remainder of your journey without further mishap," he said, and turned away. "*Au revoir, mademoiselle!*"

Still rather dazed by the whole incident, Jesamine did no more than incline her own head slightly, then watched him get back into his car and drive away. He had been brusque and arrogant, and not in the least like the traditional gallant Frenchman, but somehow he had impressed her, and she found herself wondering about him, who he was and where he had come from.

Suddenly realising where she was, she shook her head, impatient with her own bemusement, and turned to see if her own car had survived the bump as unscathed as the Mercedes had. If it had not, she would be stranded, for she had no hope of helping herself. Sliding behind the wheel, she held her breath while she tried the starter, letting it out in a deep sigh of relief when the engine whirred into life. Now that she was on her way again it should not take her long to reach Grosvallée, and she hoped for a more warm welcome at the Château d'Armor than she had received from that brusque, disturbing stranger on the road.

A breathtaking glimpse through a cluster of chestnut trees of rounded towers and slim, pointed roofs gave Jesamine her first glimpse of the Château d'Armor, and she felt her heart give a skip of excitement as she drove through the gateway. A curious tingling shivered along her spine, and she felt the warm flush of colour in her cheeks as she anticipated the coming interview.

A long tree-lined drive wound with leisurely grace until it broadened into a wide, gravel-covered area in front of the château, and when she stopped the engine the silence seemed to fall around her in a wave of blessed peace.

Close to, the building itself was even more delightful than she had expected from that tree-shrouded glimpse earlier and she took a second or two to admire it. Even though it was built of the local granite which lent a rather gloomy look to the château's elegant lines, it was attractive, and in her mind she hastily recalled something of its history.

The d'Armor family, she knew, had commissioned its design from one of France's most famous architects during the sixteenth century and, apart from a time following the revolution when it had stood deserted, it had been in the same family ever since. Charles Louis had escaped from here to England and founded her own family's place in history.

The current head of the family was François d'Armor, although he was now eighty-eight years old and the reins of the family vineyards and the wine business were in the hands of his grandson, Paul d'Armor. Old François's wife, Clothilde, was also alive, though now in her eighties, but their only daughter, Louise, had been killed during the last war.

It was of Louise d'Armor that Jesamine thought now, as she sat in her car still, for there seemed to be several facts that were puzzling about her. Her death had apparently been something of a mystery, also there seemed to be no report of her ever having married, although she was the mother of Paul d'Armor. All these facts combined to arouse Jesamine's journalistic interest, although she had not come, she reminded herself, to cause anyone any unhappiness by raking over too recent history.

Since there was little else to do, she left her car where it was and climbed the wide stone steps to the iron-studded door, then hesitated for a moment before she rang the bell. There was a strange uneasiness in her suddenly, and she looked up at the elegant, peaceful façade of the château with eyes that were darkened with doubt.

It was ridiculous, of course it was, to feel so uneasy, and she jolted herself out of her indecision, reminding herself briskly that she had a job to do. Her summons on the big iron bell pull beside the door was answered with such promptness that she almost suspected someone had been waiting for her to ring, and she smiled a little uncertainly at the woman who answered it.

The woman was in her sixties, Jesamine guessed, and she had iron grey hair and eyes that were as bright as dark buttons in an incredibly plain face. She looked at Jesamine with a frankly curious look and raised sparse brows in enquiry. "*Oui, mademoiselle?*" she asked.

Jesamine produced a card with her name on it and handed it over. "Monsieur d'Armor is expecting me," she said, and repeated her name so that there should be no misunderstanding. "My name is Arden, Jesamine Arden."

"Ah, *mais oui*, Mademoiselle Arden!" The woman stood back, apparently satisfied that she was who she claimed to be, and opening the door a little wider to admit her. "Monsieur le Comte expects you!"

The grandeur of the title surprised Jesamine for the minute, for she had studied her subject as well as was possible and there was no record of the present head of the family using his legally obsolete title. It was little use questioning the woman about it, however, but she made a note to raise the matter with François d'Armor himself.

The interior of the château was every bit as delightful as its external design had suggested it would be. Tall, slim windows balanced the wide hall and gave it grace and proportion, while a curved white stone staircase followed the elegant curves of the semi-circular hall, with its domed ceiling and gilded relief of garlands of vine leaves and grapes.

One or two paintings on the walls caught her eye as she followed the woman across the tiled hall, and she could not decide why the strong expressive faces reminded her of someone. It came as such a shock when it did occur to her that she stopped and stared at the portrait of an eighteenth-century gentleman in pale blue silk. With a very few changes it could have been a portrait of her own grand-father as a young man, and this first link in the chain thrilled her as nothing had ever done before.

"Mademoiselle?"

She brought herself hastily back to earth when she realised that the woman was watching her, looking back with her bright, button eyes and holding open a door – apparently leading into one of the rooms off the hall. The look in the woman's eyes told her that she knew well enough who she was and why she was there, and she smiled and pointed to the painting.

"Who is this?" she asked, and the woman did not even need to look at the portrait as she answered. Obviously she was well informed about her employer's family and, Jesamine suspected, would be jealous in protecting their interests.

"Monsieur Charles Louis Vernais, Comte d'Armor," she told her, and the name flowed easily off her tongue, as if it too was too familiar to need thought.

Jesamine looked again at the picture, feeling a strange sense of occasion as she stood face to face with her gallant but mysterious ancestor at last. If the likeness was a true one, there was little doubt that Mistress Louise Sutton would have found him irresistible.

"Mademoiselle, s'il vous plaît!" Once more that reproving voice prompted her from across the hall, and she smiled apologetically as she hurried across to the open door. Those bright eyes questioned her curiously as she walked past her and into the room, and the woman's voice sounded vaguely disapproving. "Mademoiselle Jesamine Arden, Monsieur le Comte," she announced, and withdrew at once, leaving Jesamine standing just inside a huge, shadowed room that took her breath away.

It could have changed little since it was first designed, she thought, for the furniture was slim and elegant, too ornate for modern taste but perfect in this big, elegant room with its huge mirrors and crystal chandeliers. The fireplace was enormous and screened in this warm summer weather with a tapestry screen of immense proportions that depicted the château itself in an earlier age, with a hunt emerging from the trees.

The figure in the armchair by the fireplace startled her at first, and she felt her heart hammering anxiously in her breast as she walked forward. A lot depended upon the first impression she made on François d'Armor, she realised, and she guessed it must be he.

Her first impression of him was one of disappointment, for she found it hard to see the man before her as descended directly from that elegant, silken-suited gallant in the hall. François d'Armor was eighty-eight years old, she knew, but he looked every year of it, and he was so small and shrunken that she felt more pity in the first instance than the excitement she had expected.

He had a small, lined face that looked out from below thin white hair and sparse brows like thin white lines above dark, bright eyes, the most lively feature in the whole face. His hands were small too and looked as if they had little flesh left on their fragile bones, and from the waist down his body was swathed in a dark blue rug, so that he had a curiously doll-like appearance.

"Mademoiselle Arden!" A wrinkled hand signalled her to come closer and Jesamine obeyed its command, drawn by those dark, bright eyes that smiled at her from the drawn features. "I am François d'Armor," he said, extending the same hand to her. "*Bienvenue*, Mademoiselle Arden! Do not heed the formality of Brigitte, *s'il vous plaît*," he added with a light shrug of his thin shoulders. "The title is as dead as the days that created it!"

He was charming, Jesamine decided with relief. No matter if he was over eighty years old, he was gallant in the old tradition, and she was not altogether surprised when he conveyed her hand briefly to his lips. "I'm delighted to meet you, Monsieur d'Armor," she said, and sat, as he indicated she should, in one of the gilt chairs close to his own.

"*Je vous demand pardon*," the old man apologised as she sat down. "I am seldom able to leave this chair – I hope you will forgive me, *mademoiselle*!"

"Oh, but of course, *monsieur*," she told him with a smile. "I'm only sorry for your sake."

"*Vous êtes bien aimable*," François d'Armor murmured. "And now, *mademoiselle*, has your journey been pleasant? You are not too wearied?"

"Not at all," Jesamine assured him. "The only unpleasant thing was that my photographer friend caught a virus of some kind and I've had to leave him in a hospital in Nantes, though not for long, I hope. The journey here was lovely and I thoroughly enjoyed driving through your beautiful countryside."

"*Bien!*" Her appreciation of the country obviously pleased him. "The traffic was not too – busy?" he asked, and Jesamine was again reminded of that other and far less gallant Frenchman she had met along the road.

"I'm afraid I had a little trouble just before I got here," she told him, pulling a rueful face. "I took a corner too sharply and almost had an accident."

The old man looked concerned. "Oh, *mademoiselle*," he said anxiously. "You were not harmed?"

"I wasn't hurt," Jesamine assured him, "only my dignity, Monsieur d'Armor! The man I collided with wasn't as gallant as I'd always been led to expect of your countrymen and he left me in no doubt that the whole thing was my fault!"

"But this is *terrible, mademoiselle!*" He raised his fragile-looking hands in horror at his countryman's shortcomings, and shook his head. "What an impression you must have gained of us!"

"Not at all," Jesamine denied smilingly. "I think I was just unfortunate to have met the exception that proves the rule!"

"*Merci*," he said, "you are too kind, *mademoiselle!* It is possible, Mademoiselle Arden, that this so ungallant young man was one of those accustomed to the company of – *femmes liberées*. There are many courtesies to be lost in such changes, *n'est-ce pas?*"

"Possibly," Jesamine, not prepared to commit herself, nor yet to openly disagree with her host.

"Ah, now! When you are suitably refreshed and rested after your journey," the old man said, wisely not pressing the point, "we will speak of family matters, hmm?"

"It's why I'm here," said Jesamine, and he nodded.

"But first you will take some tea in the English fashion?" he suggested with a twinkle. His laughter surprised her, and she wondered if he really was as frail as he appeared, or whether it was a triumph over adversity, and the spirit of François d'Armor was stronger than the body that housed it. "You see we are prepared for you!" he told her, and indicated a long gold tassel to one side of the fireplace. "If you will be so kind as to ring for Brigitte, *mademoiselle!*"

It was obvious, a few moments later, that the call had been expected, for the door opened to admit not only the same grey-haired woman who had admitted her, but another woman, tall, white-haired and evidently less sure about extending the same warmth of welcome that François d'Armor had.

He stretched out a hand to her as she came across the room and Jesamine watched her surreptitiously while the housekeeper wheeled a trolley of tea and petits fours into place in front of her. A tall figure, yet somehow fragile, as if her eighty odd years weighed heavily on her.

"*Mon amie,*" the old man said as she joined him, "*je vous présente* Mademoiselle Jesamine Arden; *mademoiselle, je vous présente* Madame Clothilde d'Armor, my wife."

"Madame d'Armor!" Jesamine took the proffered hand and found it cool and dry, the eyes that looked at her briefly, anxious and uncertain, and the latter fact puzzled her to some extent.

"*Mademoiselle.*" She indicated that she should be seated again, and sat down beside her husband. "You will take tea?"

"Yes, thank you, *madame!*"

She studied her hostess as best she could from below discreetly lowered lids and decided that Madame d'Armor was a striking woman, even in old age, and she must once have been quite a beauty. Even though her uneasiness was recognisable, it did nothing to mar her elegant good manners and, given time, Jesamine decided, she could find her as charming as her husband.

The tea was thin and fragrant and drunk from tiny, delicate Sèvres porcelain cups which Jesamine was almost afraid to handle, and while they drank tea and ate the delicious petits fours Madame d'Armor seemed to relax a little. It was almost as if she had dreaded meeting her, but now that she had she was in some way reassured. Perhaps, Jesamine mused, it had something to do with the mysterious life and death of Louise d'Armor, her daughter, although Jesamine had given no indication that her interest lay in that direction.

Later the sharp-eyed Brigitte showed Jesamine to her room, when the almost ceremonial little tea-party was over, and for the first time she realised just how fortunate she was to be actually staying in the château. Her windows looked out over the lush Breton countryside, and the acres of grapevines strung like screens of green leaves across the stony fields.

A narrow river, or perhaps it was no more than a stream, ran along the foot of the sloping gardens, glinting in the sunlight and shaded over here and there by willows and chestnut trees as it wound through the extensive grounds. It was all lush and beautiful and must have cost a great deal to maintain, she thought.

No matter if Charles Louis Vernais had fled to England as a penniless refugee, his descendants must by now be as wealthy as ever their aristocratic forebears had been, and she considered the inheritance of Paul d'Armor, the one member of the family she had yet to meet.

Bathed and refreshed, she changed her clothes and prepared to join her hosts for dinner, wondering if she would meet Paul d'Armor this time. She had her own picture of him that had nothing to do with the portraits of his ancestors that hung on all the walls. A shortish man, she imagined, with dark eyes like his grandfather and perhaps a moustache, and charming, of course.

Living in style in a French château was something new

to her, but she had no intention of being overawed by it, and she looked at her reflection in a full-length mirror with a critical eye. Blue had always suited her and lent more colour to her eyes, and the hyacinth blue dress she wore gave her a softly feminine look that was bound to please her host, if his implied dislike of the liberated woman was any indication.

She checked her slim legs for unexpected ladders, then walked across and opened the door. There was no one about on the long landing, or gallery, that she could see, but she could just hear voices coming from somewhere downstairs and as she started down the ornate curved staircase, someone came out of one of the rooms.

One look at the top of his head was enough for Jesamine to recognise him and she caught her breath as she came to a sudden halt part way down, her heart suddenly hammering frantically hard at her ribs. She thought of all the trouble she had taken to make sure she neither said nor did anything to spoil François d'Armor's impression of her, and now here she was faced with the man who had left her in no doubt that he considered her something of a fool. A man, what's more, whom she had described to her host as an ungallant oaf, lacking in the manners she expected of the traditional Frenchman.

He looked up while she still stood there on the stairway, and she saw the quick flicker of surprise in those steely grey eyes when he recognised her. He was so obviously waiting for her to come all the way down that she had little option but to do as he expected, but she felt the warmth of colour that flushed her cheeks as he watched her.

"*Bonsoir, mademoiselle!*"

She had little doubt who he was from his air of confidence, and she could have sworn that it was a glint of laughter she saw in his eyes as he looked at her. He took her hand, enfolding it in his own large strong one and his fingers squeezed hers slightly, a look in his eyes that challenged her to object to the familiarity.

"I am Paul d'Armor," he told her with a slight bob of his head over the hand he still held. "We meet again, *mademoiselle* – an unexpected pleasure!"

CHAPTER TWO

KNOWING just how and where to begin an interview was not usually so difficult for her, but in this instance Jesamine felt the need to do rather more than simply ask the usual superficial questions about the character concerned. She wanted to get to know the present-day people too and learn about them. It was a much more personal matter than anything she had done before and she wanted to become more involved.

So far the impression she had received was that, although old François d'Armor welcomed her presence there, both Madame Clothilde d'Armor and her grandson would have preferred her at a greater distance. They both treated her with politeness, but there was an unmistakable something in their manner that left her in little doubt that they did not enjoy the idea of a stranger in their midst.

As if they had something to hide, she thought, and once more her thoughts went instinctively to Louise d'Armor, her hosts' only child and the mother of Paul. She had no doubt that Brigitte, the housekeeper, could have been a rich source of information if only she could have broken through that barrier of suspicion, but Brigitte was, if anything, even less inclined to unbend than Madame d'Armor herself. She did not approve of strangers, and particularly journalists, poking into family affairs, and she made no secret of it.

Jesamine had slept well after an excellent dinner and an enjoyable evening, but it had been spent discussing her own family rather than that of her hosts, so she was no better informed this morning than she had been when she arrived. François d'Armor had expressed such interest in her grandfather's years in the Merchant Navy that she had found herself recounting some of the more colourful exploits told to her by her grandfather, and the subject of Charles Louis Vernais had barely been touched upon.

Madame d'Armor had said little, but she had appeared quite interested, and it seemed to Jesamine that the old lady became less wary of her as the evening wore on, and for that she was thankful. She had high hopes of a closer rapport with her, perhaps a contribution in the form of the woman's view of the romance she was investigating.

Paul d'Armor had left them soon after dinner, and shortly afterwards Jesamine had heard a car drive off and assumed he was spending the rest of the evening in more convivial company. It was not difficult to guess that there was a woman somewhere in the background, perhaps more than one, for a man as attractive and virile as Paul d'Armor was unlikely to be short of feminine admirers, she guessed, and she wondered idly why he had never married.

She took one more look out of her bedroom windows before she went downstairs, and made a vow to explore at least some of the acres around the château before she left for home. Charles Louis Vernais must often have ridden and walked in those lovely grounds, and they were surely a link with him that had changed little since his day. The hunting scene depicted on the firescreen downstairs, she recalled, had been easily recognisable.

Her first task must be to learn more about the man himself, for he was the pivot on which the whole of her story turned, and on her way downstairs the following morning she paused in the hall to gaze once more at his portrait – the man in the blue silk suit, who had wooed and won an English squire's daughter and so forged a link between her own family and the aristocratic d'Armors.

She found him fascinating for more reason than that he

24

was her ancestor. He had a look about him that was oddly and disturbingly reminiscent of someone else, and yet was nothing to do with his likeness to her grandfather. It was a certain look in the painted eyes, that had been so expertly captured by the artist, and a suggestion of arrogance in the angle of the head. Something challenging that stirred a flutter of recognition in her but as yet refused to be identified. Looking at him aroused all kinds of sensations that both puzzled her and made her uneasy.

"*Bonjour, mademoiselle!*"

At the sound of a voice immediately behind her, Jesamine swung round hastily and found herself looking into the steel-grey eyes of Paul d'Armor. It was in that moment that she recognised that challenging gaze of Charles Louis Vernais, for, apart from their difference in colour, the two pairs of eyes held exactly the same expression.

The blue silk and creamy lace of the eighteenth century had given way to a light grey shirt, fitted closely across a broad chest and shoulders, and slim-hipped grey slacks with wide bottoms, but the air of self-assurance was still there, undiminished by the centuries, and she found herself as much disturbed by the modern man as by the image of his aristocratic forebear.

How easy it must have been, she thought a little dizzily, for the arrogant, compelling Frenchman to turn Louise Sutton's quiet world upside down. She was experiencing much the same kind of reaction herself, and she was far more wordly than a country squire's daughter would have been.

"Good morning, Monsieur d'Armor." Her voice, she realised, sounded oddly breathless, and she was appalled to notice it. It was only to be hoped that Paul d'Armor would not do so too.

"You were admiring the last Comte d'Armor?" he asked,

and Jesamine nodded.

"Yes, I was," she agreed. "He must have been a very fascinating man, judging by his portrait."

"Ah!" She would have sworn there was a hint of satisfaction in the barely audible exclamation, and she wondered if he was himself aware of his likeness to Charles Louis. "Then you also find him – *séduisant, mademoiselle*?"

There was a hint of mockery in his eyes as well as that unmistakable challenge and, although she did not know exactly what *séduisant* meant, she had a good enough idea for her to nod her head. She was ready to admit that their mutual forebear would have had no more difficulty in seducing an inexperienced country girl like Louise Sutton than his modern counterpart would.

"I've no doubt he was a very attractive man," she said, "and Louise must have found him quite irresistible in the circumstances. He would be something quite – quite different from what she was used to in a small English village."

"The traditional romantic Frenchman, *n'est-ce pas, mademoiselle*?" Paul d'Armor mocked, soft-voiced. "And you share the taste of your impressionable ancestor?"

Realising suddenly that he was laughing at her was something of a shock, and Jesamine caught her breath sharply. Laughter glittered unmistakably in his eyes and lent a suggestion of cruelty to his wide and rather sensual mouth as he looked at her, and she felt a warm flush of colour in her cheeks as she lifted her chin. It was not easy to meet the mockery in his eyes, but she held his gaze determinedly and with far more boldness than she felt.

"Apparently I do, Monsieur d'Armor!" she said. "Although the traditional gallant Frenchman is a dying race, it seems!"

She had meant the jibe to go home and she saw the swift flick of one brow, as if her response was unexpected, and he

26

watched her steadily, his fair head angled in the same arrogant way as the man in the portrait, his mouth curved into a half smile.

"You do not speak French, of course, *mademoiselle*," he remarked, and from his tone it was evident that he considered it a defect in her make-up. "It is evident from the way in which you pronounce my name," he explained without giving her time to reply, and Jesamine frowned.

She could find nothing wrong with the way she pronounced his name, and no one else had complained. Having her accent criticised so pointedly on her first morning there was not a good beginning, she felt, and she was instinctively on the defensive. It occurred to her that possibly this was to be his way of discouraging an unwelcome visitor, but if it was then he would find her not so easily discouraged, and she faced up to him squarely, questioning his criticism.

"I wasn't aware of anything wrong with my pronunciation of your name, *monsieur*," she told him. "Monsieur François d'Armor hasn't mentioned it, and I've been pronouncing it the same way ever since yesterday!"

"I observed as much during dinner last evening." Paul d'Armor remarked coolly. "You consistently used the expression for, 'of love', but I refrained from commenting at that time because you were a dinner guest and there at Grandpère's invitation."

"I see!" She was prepared to argue his grandfather's right to invite her, had he raised the question, but he did not. Instead he continued, as if she had not spoken.

"This morning, however," he went on, "I realise that it is possible you will remain our guest for several days, and I cannot tolerate hearing myself wrongly addressed for an indefinite period. Our name is d'Armor, *mademoiselle*, not *d'amour* – the 'r' is pronounced!"

"I'm grateful for your instruction, *monsieur*!"

27

She had meant her remark to be sarcastic, but either he did not recognise the fact, or he chose to ignore it. "Then will you oblige me by using the correct pronunciation, *s'il vous plaît, mademoiselle?*" he suggested, soft-voiced, and his grey eyes noted her flushed cheeks and glittered a challenge. "Grandpère is too gallant to correct you," he added smoothly, "I am not!"

"I'd noticed *that*, Monsieur d'Armor!" Jesamine told him shortly. She resented the effect of those grey eyes almost more than she did his correcting her, and she had seldom felt more uncertain of herself before. It was not a sensation she enjoyed. "I apologise for my accent," she went on a trifle breathlessly, "but French is not one of my languages, as I told you yesterday!"

"Ah, *mais oui!*" He seemed to find the recollection amusing, for he was smiling, and she remembered a similar smile when he had lectured her yesterday on the dangers of driving on the wrong side of the road. "You refer to our meeting on the Grosvallée road, *n'est-ce pas?*" he asked.

"When you accused me of driving on the wrong side of the road," Jesamine said. "Which I wasn't!"

"No?" He laughed shortly and shook his head.

"No!" Jesamine insisted firmly. "I explained how that happened, Monsieur d'Armor—I almost missed my turning and took the corner wide." She looked at him reproachfully, and the small pout she made was quite unconscious. "I was quite shaken by that near collision!"

"And you thought me a *brute sans coeur*, hmm? he guessed, apparently unconcerned. "Because I asked you for assistance in freeing my *auto!*"

"And which I gave willingly once I knew what I had to do!" she reminded him.

"So you did, *mademoiselle!*"

He was regarding her again with that same frankly

speculative glow in his eyes that she had seen yesterday, and she turned hastily back to her study of the portrait. She found Charles Louis infinitely less disturbing at the moment than his descendant.

"I'm not a mechanic," she said, without looking at him.

"*Mais non, mademoiselle!*"

Once more she suspected he was laughing at her and she looked over her shoulder at him, her eyes bright and resentful. "I even hurt my hand on your wretched car," she complained, and extended her hand with a bruise still faintly visible across her knuckles.

Before she could withdraw it he reached out and took her hand in his own hard, strong fingers, looked at it for a second or two, then conveyed it to his lips. The warm pressure of his mouth on her fingers was so unexpected that it set the blood pounding in her head and she did nothing for several seconds but stare at the top of his bowed head.

"Monsieur d'Armor," she said, but he raised his head then and she fell silent once more.

"You thought me ungallant, *mademoiselle*," he reminded her. "I must try to remedy that."

The eyes that watched her seemed much too brightly glistening to be apologetic and Jesamine shook her head, suspecting mockery. "Please don't bother, Monsieur d'Armor," she told him. "As a journalist I'm quite used to a certain amount of—" She shrugged, unwilling to openly accuse him of chauvinism. "Besides," she added, "I'm here to write the story of Charles Louis Vernais, not to be concerned with your lack of gallantry, Monsieur d'Armor."

Paul d'Armor looked at the portrait for a second, one brow raised queryingly. "Does not *his* lack of gallantry concern you, *mademoiselle?*" he asked, and she too glanced briefly at the portrait. "He did not marry the lady," he reminded her, "even though she was—" Expressive hands

29

conveyed Louise Sutton's delicate condition at the time of Charles Louis's departure, and Jesamine shook her head.

She turned yet again and looked up at the strong, arrogant features of their mutual forebear, but she was even more tinglingly aware of the latest of his line standing immediately behind her. She would have to keep her rather disturbing awareness of Paul d'Armor firmly under control if she was to do her job properly. Her present sensitivity was something new to her and she disliked its effect on her normally clear-headed character.

"Has it never occurred to anyone that he might not have known anything about the child?" she asked.

In her mind she had already written the feature as the tender and touching romance of two young lovers, parted by circumstances beyond their control, and she disliked having Paul d'Armor suggesting that his ancestor had been doing nothing more than amusing himself while in a foreign land. It reduced her romantic theory to a mere sordid episode, hardly worthy of note, and she refused to see it as no more than that.

Paul d'Armor's grey eyes watched her steadily with a hint of malice that suggested he knew what her own theory was and would delight in proving her wrong. "Has it occurred to you, *mademoiselle*," he said quietly, "that he did not care?"

"No!"

He raised a brow at her vehement denial. "You feel you know him so well?" he asked.

"I feel I know him better than that!" she retorted, determined to stick to her guns. She looked again at Charles Louis and met the same dark, mocking look in his brown eyes that she saw in Paul d'Armor's grey ones. It gave her a qualm of uncertainty, but she refused to recognise it.

"I believe I know him better, *mademoiselle*!" he said,

and Jesamine looked at him once more, trying in her mind to dissociate the two characters—that of the man in the portrait and the one beside her. It was incredibly difficult to do, much more difficult than she would have believed.

"And you—you think he would have deserted her?" she asked, doubt making her sound uncertain at last. "You think he'd have come back to France and left her, knowing she was having his child?" She looked at him steadily, as if his morals were in question rather than those of a man long dead. But somehow she felt he would know exactly why Charles Louis had acted the way he did. "Would you?" she asked a little breathlessly, and he did not reply at once.

Then a faint smile tugged at one corner of his mouth and he shrugged lightly. "It is not I who has to answer your charge, *mademoiselle*," he told her. "And he is not here to be judged!"

"No." She looked up at the portrait and sighed, trying to keep her mind on history rather than the man who stood beside her.

"You find him wanting?" Paul d'Armor suggested, and she would have denied it hastily, but then she was unsure whether Charles Louis Vernais was any different from the way she had always pictured him. A rogue perhaps, but a charming and attractive one who must have found little Louise Sutton an easy conquest. "You are not sure!" he said, and once more his smile mocked her.

"No, I'm not sure," Jesamine admitted, instinctively on the defensive. "Women will forgive a man like—like him a great deal, and even a country girl like Louise Sutton must have known that she was playing with fire when she took him for her lover! Just the same—"

"You would like to have known him!" Paul d'Armor guessed, and her look dared him to find that amusing.

"I mean to know him before I leave here, Monsieur d'Armor," she told him. "He and Louise Sutton are the main characters in my story, but he, I think, will be the more interesting of the two from the reader's point of view." She sighed again for the task ahead of her. "For one thing," she said, "why, if he was called Vernais, do you—your family use the name d'Armor?"

She did not really expect him to answer, for she expected little or no help from him if his attitude so far was any indication. It would not have surprised her if he had simply shrugged off the question. Instead he answered her without hesitation, albeit rather shortly.

"Because it is our name by right, *mademoiselle*," he told her. "When he—Charles Louis Vernais, returned to France, he was destitute, deprived of everything but his pride and, since he was not allowed to use his title for fear of his life, he made it his name. When Henri, his son, contrived to regain the lands and the house many years later he continued to be known as d'Armor, and it has remained so ever since."

Jesamine was interested, even intrigued, and she could not deny that she found the fact of Paul d'Armor being her informant even more intriguing. In fact there was a sense of satisfaction about his having volunteered the information. "I see," she said, turning to face him once more. "So to all intents the title is still yours!"

"*Précisément!*" The grey eyes quizzed her narrowly for a second. "You perhaps think it false pride, *mademoiselle*?" he suggested, but went on without giving her time to answer the challenge. "Do you know that the original name for Brittany was Armor?" he asked, and Jesamine shook her head. "We are a very old family, *mademoiselle*, you must allow us our pride!"

"Oh, but of course I do," Jesamine assured him. "In

fact I suppose I could feel some of the same pride myself, since we share a mutual ancestor."

That had been reckless of her, Jesamine recognised that even before she finished speaking. She should not have laid such determined claim to kinship with the proud and wealthy d'Armors. Paul d'Armor would dislike such presumption, possibly more than anyone, being the man he was. He was looking at her now with a steady and disturbing gaze, much as he might have regarded a specimen of lower life who had dared to presume kinship.

"Your own frail connection scarcely warrants it, *mademoiselle*," he observed. "The liáison, although productive, was, I beg leave to assume, no more than casual, and Mademoiselle Sutton's *enfant d'amour* never bore our name!"

His disclaimer was even more harsh than she had expected and Jesamine felt the flush of colour flood her cheeks. "I believe he loved her!" she insisted, refusing to abandon her romantic theory in favour of his more earthy one. "I'm *sure* he must have loved her!"

One light brow expressed vague amusement at her romantic supposition, and Paul d'Armor's eyes gleamed. "Hence your insistence on *d'amour* instead of d'Armor?" he suggested, and laughed softly. "How *romantique, mademoiselle*!"

Jesamine said nothing for a moment. She stood facing him with her eyes downcast while she struggled with the beginnings of a temper that could be quite formidable if she was pushed too far. She had no wish to begin her stay like this, by crossing swords with old François's grandson, but she could hardly stand there and let him make fun of her the way he was.

"You seem determined to be unfriendly towards me, Monsieur d'Armor," she told him, after a moment or two, "and I can't think why."

Her voice was not as steady as she would have liked, and possibly he suspected it was caused by approaching tears rather than the anger that really motivated it. For he put a hand under her chin suddenly and she almost flinched from the strong fingers that lifted her face to him so that the steel grey eyes searched her face slowly for a second or two before he spoke.

"I am not unfriendly, *mademoiselle*," he said, in a voice that was much softer and lower in pitch than he more normally used. "I merely wished to point out to you that a casual *affaire* is not of necessity an *affaire de coeur*."

Jesamine was trembling, and the knowledge that it was something to do with Paul d'Armor holding her the way he was, not only amazed her but annoyed her too, and she drew back from that strong but strangely gentle hand, looking up at him with bright, defiant eyes.

"I assume you make the observation from experience of both, *monsieur*," she said pertly, "since you speak with such confidence!"

She saw the gleam that betrayed anger, but it showed only briefly then his eyes glistened with that disturbing laughter again, and she hastily lowered her own gaze. "Did you doubt it, *mademoiselle*?" he challenged.

All day Jesamine spent time making notes, building up a background. She had walked down to the little village of Grosvallée and sat for a while beside the same stream that ran at the bottom of the grounds of the Château d'Armor. So far she had spoken to no one except to acknowledge a few friendly '*bonjours*' as she passed by, aware that the eyes of men and women alike followed her progress with interest.

It was interesting to speculate how much the people in the village could have told her about the more recent history of the d'Armor family, but she had no intention of

34

prying into things that did not concern her and possibly raising discomfiting ghosts.

Her reason for staying out of the house for most of the day, she admitted, was to avoid seeing too much of Paul d'Armor, for she found him the most disturbing man she had ever met, and she resented the effect he had on her without being quite sure why. He was not good-looking, and he was more mature than most of the men of her acquaintance, but there remained that disturbing, sensual aura of challenge. It made her not only alarmingly aware of him as a man, but wary too, in case he should suspect how she felt.

She knew that during the week he would be spending most of his time in the vineyards or the cellars, so she would not have to contend with his disturbing presence. On Sunday, it seemed, her only escape was to go out herself, for he had not left the house all day.

She found herself facing him across the dinner table, but had managed to engage his grandfather's attention for most of the meal, so that she could in part ignore the ever alert grey eyes that occasionally caught hers and narrowed briefly with silent speculation.

The meal over, they sat in the big bright *salon*, good food and wine having induced a state of pleasant euphoria in which everyone was more relaxed. Jesamine, seated beside old François, tried not to look at his grandson, but inevitably her gaze was drawn to him, sitting beside his grandmother on the elegant gilded sofa.

The old man had invited her to sit near him so that they could talk more easily, and she had no objection at all, except that from there she had Paul constantly in sight. He looked arrogantly at ease with his long legs crossed one over the other, and his grey eyes narrowed against the smoke from a cigarette.

A cream shirt seemed to blend rather than contrast with his tanned face and neck, and a light grey, expensively tailored suit emphasised the broadness of his shoulders and the rangy leanness of the rest of his body. Since they left the dining table he had never once looked at her, and yet Jesamine sensed his awareness of her and shivered inwardly.

"You will, of course, know more about Mademoiselle Sutton than we do, *mademoiselle*." François d'Armor's voice brought her hastily back to earth, and Jesamine shook her head.

"I'm afraid not, Monsieur d'Armor," she denied, careful to give the name its correct pronunciation. "Sad to say she wasn't really important enough to warrant having her history recorded – we don't even have a picture of her."

"*C'est dommage*," the old man said, shaking his head. "It would have been interesting to see this lady whose love brought our two families together, *n'est-ce pas?*"

"It would," Jesamine agreed. "But actually the only written recollection we have of her is in the diaries of my great-great-grandfather, James Warden. He was Louise Sutton's great-grandson and he apparently took an interest in the family history. It was through him that we heard of her at all. He discovered the miniature in an attic, according to his diaries, along with a box of love letters. It was the letters, apparently, that gave the first indication that Louise had never married and that her child, her only child, was her lover's."

"*D'amour!*" Paul d'Armor murmured, and Jesamine flushed when she recalled their conversation that morning.

"As you say, *monsieur*!" she retorted, but hastily avoided his eyes.

François d'Armor looked momentarily puzzled by the brief exchange, then shrugged, apparently having more immediate things on his mind. "You speak of a miniature,

Mademoiselle Arden," he reminded her. "Of whom was it a likeness, if not of the lady herself?"

"Of Charles Louis Vernais," Jesamine told him. "My grandfather remembers seeing it when he was a boy, but he can't remember what eventually happened to it. Possibly it was sold some time during the early nineteen-hundreds, when the old family house was sold, Grampy doesn't remember. It definitely isn't in the family now, or I'd have discovered it while I was looking for background for this article."

"*Une dommage,*" François d'Armor said, shaking his head, and Jesamine could only agree with him.

Madame d'Armor, she realised suddenly, was looking curiously interested in the subject, and every so often she was glancing across at Jesamine, as if something about her was puzzling. It was several seconds before she said what it was, and then she mentioned it only cautiously, as if she was unsure of her ground.

"You speak of a miniature, *mademoiselle,*" she said in her quiet voice, "which was presumably given by Charles Louis Vernais to Mademoiselle Sutton. Is it not so that sometimes – lovers exchanged such likenesses? As mementoes, *n'est-ce pas? Souvenirs d'amour, oui?*"

Jesamine nodded. There was a curious fluttering sensation in her stomach that she could not quite explain as she looked across at the old lady. "Why, yes, Madame d'Armor," she said, "I think you're right. They exchanged miniatures as people today exchange photographs."

"Then perhaps," Madame d'Armor suggested, "there were – how do you say? – a pair of these miniatures exchanged." She was looking at her husband and one elegant hand indicated that he should take a look at Jesamine sitting beside him. "*Regarde Mademoiselle,*" she told him, and François frowned for a moment curiously.

37

Then he did as he was asked and turned his dark curious eyes on Jesamine and studied her for a moment. She saw realisation come suddenly in a bright glitter of expression, and he raised his hands. "*Mais oui!*" he said, his voice sharp with excitement. "*Mais oui, mon amie,* you are right, so right!"

Jesamine looked from one to the other curiously, that flutter of excitement now more urgent than ever, and she felt Paul's eyes on her too suddenly, narrowed and glistening. He was smiling too, showing strong white teeth in that craggy face, and her heart gave a sudden lurch as she met his gaze briefly.

"Ah *mais oui, naturellement,* Grandmama!" he said. "*La fille de la nuit.* The dark girl," he translated for Jesamine's benefit, "with the face of an angel!"

His grandmother looked momentarily startled at his extravagant compliment, but she nodded as if she found it apt, and smiled at him. "Perhaps Mademoiselle Arden would like to see it," she suggested tentatively, and Paul was already on his feet before she had finished speaking, and making for the door.

"*Naturellement,* Mademoiselle must see it!" he said.

François d'Armor was nodding his head approvingly and smiling at his wife. "So clever of you to see it, *ma chère,*" he told her, and Jesamine's heart beat hard in anticipation, for she felt sure she knew what was happening, or about to happen.

"You will find *la fille de la nuit* to your liking, *mademoiselle,*" Madame d'Armor promised, and her husband looked at her with a hint of mischief in his eyes.

"This is an unexpected moment for you, *mademoiselle, n'est-ce pas*?" he asked. "But there can be no doubt at all who *la fille de la nuit* is – or was."

"I can still scarcely believe it," Jesamine said, and

laughed a little unsteadily. "It's marvellous to think that a picture of Louise exists after all. I didn't expect anything like this!"

"She has hung in the small *salon* for many years," François told her. "We did not know who she was but she was so – *très jolie* that we had not the heart to part with her!" He inclined his head in his grandson's direction when Paul returned carrying a tiny gilt frame in one large hand. "*Regardez, ma chère!*"

The gilt frame contained a miniature painted in soft, glowing colours, and when Paul handed it to her he leaned his weight on the arm of her chair so that his face was close beside her own, and she felt her senses respond when she was enveloped in the warmth of his body as he leaned even closer to point to the small painted face surrounded by a cloud of dark hair. She found it hard to concentrate, but determinedly fixed her attention on the likeness of Louise Sutton.

"The face of an angel," he murmured, "*n'est-ce pas, mademoiselle?*"

Jesamine took the miniature, her stomach curling with excitement. Louise Sutton looked to have been about eighteen years old when the picture was painted, and there was no denying she was pretty. She had large blue eyes and a look of innocence that must have appealed to the bold *chevalier* as much as her beauty.

Her dress, as much of it as was shown, was almost severe for that age. Dark blue in colour, it had a fichu of lace tied modestly over the low-cut bodice, matching the little white cap that was barely visible on the thick, dark hair. Nothing as extravagant as the richness of blue silk such as her lover affected in the portrait in the hall.

Jesamine studied her for several minutes, then she shook her head slowly. "She's pretty," she said, "but – not quite as I expected her to be."

"You are disappointed?" It was Paul d'Armor's voice that questioned her opinion and he sounded surprised.

Jesamine took a second to answer. "No," she denied at last, "not disappointed. But I feel somehow as if – " She laughed a little uncertainly. "I feel I should know her," she confessed, and the sound of Paul d'Armor's laughter mocked her uncertainty.

"*Mademoiselle*," he taunted, "do you not know your own face?"

CHAPTER THREE

IT had been Madame d'Armor's decision to hang the miniature of Louise Sutton in Jesamine's room, and the gesture had been so unexpected that it gave her double the pleasure. During the past couple of days she felt she had, to some extent, overcome the old lady's initial wariness of her and, as a consqeuence, she felt more at ease herself.

She had made little or no progress with the actual writing of the article, although she had added enormously to her knowledge of the d'Armor family history, for François d'Armor was as eloquent a story-teller as her own grandfather and she was nothing loath to sit and listen to him.

Surrounded by the elegant trappings of the Château d'Armor, it was easy to lose herself in the stories of the earlier members of its family. Bold, arrogant and romantically dashing, they seemed to fairly describe Paul d'Armor as Jesamine saw him. Only one obvious omission from the old man's narrative struck her, and that was that he made not a single mention of his only child – the other Louise, who had been Paul's mother.

The tiny portrait of Louise Sutton was hung in an alcove near the window, its detail more clearly visible in the broad light of day, and several times since it had been put there, Jesamine had taken time to study it. She had come to the conclusion, after close study of her, that possibly that large-eyed look of innocence need not be a true indication of Louise's character.

If one looked closely enough there was a certain tilt to the chin that suggested a will at least as strong as her own, and there was a steadiness about that innocent gaze that suggested more strength of character than the angelic features might at first imply.

It seemed incredible that she should have been with the d'Armor family all those years without their having had an inkling of who she really was, but at the same time it lent strength to Jesamine's theory. Charles Louis would surely never have brought the likeness of his English lover back with him and kept it for the rest of his life unless he had truly loved her. No matter what Paul d'Armor implied, Jesamine still saw them as a pair of tragic lovers parted by circumstances, and she meant to portray them as such.

She looked again at the tiny painted face surrounded by its cloud of dark hair, and speculated. The face of an angel, Paul d'Armor had described it as and, almost in the same breath, asked if she did not recognise her own face.

Of course there was a likeness, Jesamine herself had seen it, once it had been pointed out to her. Enough of a likeness for Madame d'Armor to have recognised the unknown dark girl for who she was after so many years. None of them had any doubt that *la fille de la nuit* with the face of an angel was Louise Sutton, and Jesamine speculated for a moment on whether Paul d'Armor also considered that she too had the face of an angel.

Her own likeness to Louise, and Paul d'Armor being a more fair-haired image of Charles Louis Vernais, led her to speculate in another direction too. Like whether the same situation could arise in the present circumstances if she did not guard against it, and before she turned away she reached out and touched the ornate little gilt frame with a forefinger, smiling ruefully.

"I hope I have more will-power than you had, Louise," she whispered to the girl in the portrait.

Walking across, she picked up her handbag from the bed

and glanced idly out of the window as she did so at the broad expanse of the château grounds, bright and summery in the sun. She was too preoccupied for the moment, however, to consciously notice anything, and it was only as she turned to go that she was brought sharply back to earth by the sight of Paul d'Armor.

She paused instinctively in the act of turning, to look at him, striding out across the neatly formal gardens with that long, slightly impatient stride of his and her heart missed a beat. She took the opportunity to observe him without herself being observed, for she felt sure he had not yet seen her. Standing back from the window she was half concealed by the curtains and she felt she was safe from notice while she watched him, trying to identify just what it was about him that was so irresistibly attractive.

She had known attractive men before, handsome men and younger than Paul d'Armor, but never one as capable of disturbing her emotions as he did, and the fascination he held for her also, in some way, made her resentful. He must be somewhere between thirty-five and forty, she estimated, although it was always more difficult to tell with such rugged features, and the arrogance of his manner owed itself to generations of aristocratic feudalism that would take a lot longer than two hundred years to eradicate. Paul d'Armor was an enigma, and one she felt she just had to find an answer to.

She suddenly realised he had seen her when he raised his head and looked in the direction of her window. It was a steady, imperious look, well in keeping with the character of the man, and it evoked a curious curling sensation in her stomach, so that she clenched her hands tightly as she gazed down on him.

For a moment she thought he was going to ignore her, but then he raised a hand suddenly in a careless salute, inclining his head in a brief bow when she fluttered a hand in uncertain response. It was impossible to read any expression from where she stood, and a second later he disappeared, striding out of sight below her window as she turned away.

Glancing once more at the miniature hanging in the alcove, she looked at Louise Sutton with a glimmer of understanding in her eyes. Her heart was still thudding hard in her breast and she sighed as she opened the door of her room to go downstairs. She was behaving as if she was just as impressionable as the girl in the picture, she thought despairingly, and gave herself a mental shake as she closed the door firmly behind her. She had no intention of allowing history to repeat itself.

It had rained in the night, but the morning promised to be warm and sunny and Jesamine had decided to take advantage of it and walk down to the village again. She could have driven herself, but she had always found walking conducive to mental activity, and she really must think about putting the article she was supposed to be writing into some more tangible form.

She had no particular objective in mind other than to be alone with her thoughts for a while and perhaps absorb a little atmosphere. Walking would give her some much-needed exercise too, for she had spent far too long sitting indoors during the past two days, and, pleasant as it was, she was not getting her job done.

It had not even occurred to her when she saw Paul from her bedroom window that she would probably come across him as she made her way downstairs, and the sight of him coming into the hall from the rear of the house made her hesitate only half-way down.

He came striding into the hall with the same slightly

impatient gait she had noticed from her window. A blue denim shirt with the sleeves rolled up above the elbows, and fawn slacks, were in direct contrast to the smart, formally suited image she had seen so far, but they did nothing to detract from that basic and very masculine aura about him.

In fact, in working clothes he might have looked less sophisticated, but he was much more earthily attractive, and she felt her pulses responding to him even before he looked up and saw her on the stairs and she was subjected to that steady, almost insolent scrutiny. Then his gaze shifted slightly and he noted the handbag she carried.

"You are going out, *mademoiselle*?" he asked, as if he had every right to question her movements.

"I am," she agreed.

There was a suggestion of a smile on his mouth that she instinctively mistrusted, and it gleamed in his eyes as he looked at her. "You will remember to drive on the correct side of the road?" he asked, and Jesamine bit her lip determinedly rather than make the retort she was tempted to.

"I'm not driving, *monsieur*," she told him. "I'm going for a walk."

"To the village?"

It could have been her imagination, but she thought she detected a hint of sharpness in the question, as if he disliked the idea, and she did not answer at once. There was no reason why he should suddenly take an interest in what she did, nor did he have any cause to object, and an uncontrollable niggle of suspicion made her frown at him curiously.

"I *was* thinking of going to the village, as a matter of fact," she told him, and left him in no doubt that she saw it as none of his business where she went.

The merest suggestion of tightness pulled at his wide

mouth and there was a glitter in his eyes as he stood in the middle of the hall watching her come slowly down the rest of the stairs. "My interest is practical, *mademoiselle*," he said. "I cannot imagine why you should wish to walk when you have an *auto* or why you should wish to go to the village when there are better shops only a few kilometres away."

"But I don't want shops," she informed him. "And you don't have to concern yourself with me, Monsieur d'Armor, I'm quite happy just browsing around."

"Browsing?" Obviously the word was unknown to him, and she half-smiled – his English was usually so good.

"It means that I want to look around Grosvallée," she told him, "and you don't have to be suspicious of my intentions, *monsieur*!"

He said nothing for a moment, then he inclined his head briefly, his voice coolly matter-of-fact when he spoke. "I am driving through the village on my way to see one of our neighbours," he told her. "It is some distance to walk and if you prefer not to drive, *mademoiselle*, perhaps you will allow me to drive you. My concern is for your well-being, I was not aware that I had cause to suspect your intentions!"

It was a direct challenge that was backed by the gleam in his eyes, and she felt rather as if she had been scolded for petulance. She felt foolish and angry with herself for letting him arouse such emotional reactions in her, and yet she could not resist the idea of riding with him in his car to the village, instead of walking as she had planned.

"*Mademoiselle?*"

His quiet voice roused her, brought her back to earth, and she hastily nodded her head while taking care not to look at him directly. "Thank you, Monsieur d'Armor," she said. "I can ride there and walk back – I seem to remember it's quite a long way. If you're sure it's no trouble."

46

"None, *mademoiselle*!" Once more that searching gaze swept over her. "You are ready at once?"

When she nodded agreement he held out a hand to her, and for a second only, she hesitated. His eyes held hers, steady and challenging, as if he expected her to shy away, but when she moved up beside him he merely touched the underside of her arm lightly with his fingertips. Nevertheless the light, tingling touch on her bare skin just below her elbow brought a fluttering reaction from her senses and she despaired of her own weakness as she walked across the hall with him.

It should have been so easy to have told him that she would prefer to walk. That she had planned a walk deliberately to give herself both exercise and the time to think, but somehow it had not been easy at all, and here she was sitting beside him in that same big black car she had collided with on the road coming in.

He drove well, which was no more than she expected, but she could not quite understand his continued silence and found it rather unnerving. Ever since that initial enquiry as to where she was going, she had known he was unhappy about something to do with her visiting the village, but she could not imagine why. Once or twice she glanced at him from the corners of her eyes, but the strong brown face in profile gave her no clue at all.

"This is all yours?"

She indicated the vineyards that spread out on either side of them. The vines sprawled like green webs along their supports, heavy with fruit, and the fields that sloped steeply in places and looked stony and barren at ground level. Vineyards seemed to cover the whole valley, girded round by the bright ribbon of the river, pale and bright and glinting in the sunlight.

"*Mais oui, mademoiselle*, it is all ours."

47

He seemed disinclined to answer even when she made the effort to open a conversation, and Jesamine felt oddly uneasy about it, as well as a little irritable. She looked again at the strong, disturbing face with its grey eyes and firm mouth, and frowned.

"Is something wrong, Monsieur d'Armor?" she asked, and he turned his head briefly, scanning her face with a swift, hard gaze, as if he suspected her question.

"In what way wrong, *mademoiselle*?" he asked, and Jesamine shook her head.

It was impossible to put a finger on anything specific, but something was making him silent and unresponsive, and she was almost certain that it was because she insisted on visiting the village. "I'm not sure," she confessed, "but you –" She shrugged uneasily. "Oh – maybe it's just my imagination!"

"It is possible, *mademoiselle*!"

His response angered her and she looked at him with bright glistening eyes. "You don't like me being here, do you?" she asked, rashly uncaring whether she was being rude or not. "You don't like the idea of me writing this article and you don't like me being at the château! In fact, Monsieur d'Armor, you don't like anything about me, do you?"

He brought the car to halt just where the narrow little road led into the village, and cut the engine, then turned in his seat and looked at her steadily for several seconds before he spoke. His eyes had a dark, unfathomable look that was much more disturbing than their usual bright, steely grey, and he searched her face with a gaze that seemed to go right through her.

"Do you wish me to be frank, *mademoiselle*?" he asked in a harsh flat voice, and Jesamine nodded silently. Once more that hard glittering gaze took stock of her flushed face and her hands curled involuntarily into tight fists on her lap. "I could find a great deal to – like – about you, *mademoiselle*," he told her in the same steel-edged voice, "but I would enjoy you more simply as a woman, rather than have you invade my home as an inquisitive meddler in my family affairs!"

The earthy frankness of his reply left her stunned for a moment and she shivered. She had asked for his candid opinion, she thought, but she had not expected him to be quite so frank and she felt a heady sense of excitement for a few seconds before anger flared up and smothered it.

"You're very honest!" she told him in a voice that was not quite steady. "But I'm not a – a meddler, Monsieur d'Armor, I'm simply a journalist doing a job, and I can't think why that should worry you so much! Gathering historical data on something that happened two hundred years ago can hardly be called meddling!"

"What reason do you have for coming to the village?" he asked, and for a moment she simply sat and stared at him.

"What reason?" She frowned at him curiously, still unable to fathom why it should matter so much to him. "Why – because I want to look around the place again, for one thing," she said.

"You have been here before?"

Jesamine nodded. "Once," she told him. "It seemed a nice little place and I felt it might give me atmosphere."

It would be difficult trying to explain to him how she hoped to get the feel of the place. Charles Louis Vernais must have seen the village very much as it looked now, and she felt it was a side of him she should not neglect – his relationships with the village people, but she saw Paul's eyes narrow suspiciously and it was obvious he still doubted her motives.

49

"*Atmosphère?*" He gave the word its French pronunciation and she thought that alone betrayed a certain agitation. "I would have thought you had the atmosphere you required at the château, *mademoiselle*. What can you learn of Charles Louis Vernais in the village that you cannot learn in the house where he lived?"

"Maybe nothing," Jesamine admitted, "but I'm not confined to the château, surely, *monsieur*!"

"It seems not!" The grey eyes glittered like ice, and again she shivered involuntarily.

"I might be able to learn something from another angle," she told him, trying to be reasonable and keep her temper. "I might learn something from the village people's family histories, information can come from the most unexpected sources."

"You mean to question the villagers?" he demanded, and she shrugged, inexplicably uneasy suddenly.

"You make it sound like an interrogation," she objected. "All I want to do is talk to them, tell them what I'm doing!"

"*Non!*" He spoke so sharply that Jesamine visibly started, looking at him with wide curious eyes. "You will not discuss my family with the village people!" Paul declared harshly. "I will not permit such a thing!"

"Oh, surely – " she began, but he raised a large hand and silenced her, his eyes glittering like ice as he looked down at her.

"If you persist in this – *curiosité, mademoiselle,*" he told her firmly, "I will see to it that you are no longer welcome at the Château d'Armor!"

"Oh, but you can't do that!" Jesamine protested without stopping to think that he quite probably could, and would, do just that if he made up his mind to it.

His steady gaze challenged her and his mouth had a

tight set look that suggested cruelty. "Indeed I can, *mademoiselle*!" he assured her quietly but firmly. "And I will do so without hesitation if you insist on prying into matters that do not concern you!"

Jesamine stared at him for a moment, her brows drawn. Her heart was fluttering anxiously and she thought for a moment that in her anxiety she must have misheard him. It dawned on her only after several seconds that he was not referring to, or concerned with, matters that happened two hundred years ago, but with something much more recent.

"Matters that don't concern me?" she asked in a small husky voice. "Charles Louis Vernais? I don't understand you, Monsieur d'Armor – isn't he why I'm here?"

It was obvious that in his anxiety he had said much more than he intended and she watched his expression curiously, feeling quite inexplicably sorry that he had made the slip. For several seconds, as he looked at her, she saw a kind of stunned realisation in his eyes, then he turned quickly in his seat and gazed fixedly out through the windscreen. His profile was hard and unrelenting and she guessed he was angry with his own fallibility.

"The people here can tell you nothing about him," he insisted, "and therefore it would be useless for you to make enquiries in the village, Mademoiselle Arden. I suggest that you continue as you have until now – everything relevant to Charles Louis Vernais is available to you at the château, and no one has yet refused to assist you in your enquiries, have they?"

"Oh no, of course they haven't," Jesamine agreed. "In fact you've all been very helpful and kind, and I'm grateful to you."

It was true, she had to admit. There was no real reason why she could not write an excellent article with the material she had already acquired, but this reluctance to allow

51

her to talk with the village people puzzled her and she wished she knew his reasons. He had turned in his seat again and was looking at her with that same steady, piercing gaze so that she hastily avoided his eyes.

He laid one arm along the back of her seat suddenly and leaned slightly towards her, bringing the uncompromising vigour of his body into contact with her so that she became inescapably and alarmingly aware of him. His eyes swept over her features with a slow, bold scrutiny that set her heart racing, no matter how hard she tried to control it.

"Then you have no need to seek outside help," he suggested, and Jesamine shook her head, an automatic gesture rather than a conscious one.

"Not really, I suppose," she allowed reluctantly, and he nodded, as if it was the answer he both sought and expected.

"So, Mademoiselle Jesamine," he said, "you will instead drive with me to see Monsieur Chavet, our neighbour, and then continue with your work at the Château d'Armor, hmm?"

The timbre of his voice, the deep challenging look in his eyes and that forceful body pressed just close enough to play havoc with her senses were all meant to persuade her to change her mind, she realised dazedly, and it would be so easy to succumb. Then some small warning voice reminded her that Paul d'Armor was in all probability a practised seducer, and the thought stiffened her resistance as she sought to counteract the effect he was having on her willpower.

She met that unnerving gaze with a determined steadiness and tried to control her voice. "I don't think so, *monsieur*," she said, "I'd like to take a look around the village again. I'm not here for very long, Monsieur d'Armor, and – "

"Paul," he interrupted with a hint of impatience, and the intimacy of the suggestion was so unexpected that Jesamine blinked uncomprehendingly for a second. "You will find I am referred to and addressed as Monsieur Paul," he informed her, and thus quashed her brief hope of a better understanding.

"I understand – Monsieur Paul!" Disappointment, however minor, put an edge on her voice and she suspected she was being firmly put in her place for the third time that day. "As I was saying, Monsieur Paul, I'm not here for very long, a few days at most, and I'd like to look around the village, as an interested visitor. That is, if you don't mind," she added with a touch of sarcasm that was meant as much to reinforce her own resistance as to anger him.

"And if I do?" he asked, watching her steadily.

Jesamine hastily avoided his eyes, realising how easily he could still persuade her if he put his mind to it and she did not keep a firm hold on her emotions. "Then I'll have to move out of the château and put up at the village inn!" she retorted. "Unless, of course, you hold the jurisdiction of overlord there as well!"

"If we were still overlords, *mademoiselle*," he told her harshly, "be sure I would put your more obvious attractions to good use – with or without your consent!"

Jesamine caught her breath. It was the second time he had made such an allusion to her physical attractions and she was breathtakingly aware of the bright gleam in his eyes and the hard fierceness of his body as he leaned towards her. He was hardly likely to put that forceful threat into action in a place as public as the village street, but she did not stop to consider that.

She turned quickly in her seat and pushed open the car door, then swung her legs out with more haste than elegance and stood on the narrow footpath. Slamming the car door, she stood looking at him, her breathing short and erratic, a dark sheen of emotion in her blue eyes.

Paul did not drive off, as she half expected him to, but sat watching her with a curious intensity that she found infinitely disturbing, and she tried once more to discover just what it was about Paul d'Armor that could affect her so deeply. It was obvious that he had expected her to let herself be persuaded, just as it was obvious he did not want her talking to the village people. She had little doubt that his reluctance in some way concerned his mother, Louise d'Armor, but surely his anxiety concealed more than the fact that she already suspected – that Louise d'Armor had never married.

Whatever his reasons, she could do nothing about her sudden urge to reassure him that her only interest was in Charles Louis Vernais, and she shook her head slowly as she tried to tell him so. "Monsieur – Paul." The grey eyes did little to encourage her, but she pressed on. "I – I really have no intention of – prying into anything that concerns you or your family. My only interest is in Charles Louis Vernais and I promise you he's the *only* one I shall ask about. I thought perhaps if I visited the church – parish registers can be – "

"No doubt, *mademoiselle*," he interrupted shortly, "but you will not find the *famille* d'Armor buried in the village church ground."

"Oh, I see!"

He did not enlighten her as to where they might be found, and she had not the nerve to ask him in the circumstances. Her silence might have told him that she was curious, but he would do nothing voluntarily to satisfy her curiosity, she knew, and while she still stood there, hesitating, he half turned in his seat and inclined his head briefly, his hands already on the wheel again.

"It seems I cannot influence you," he told her, and she suspected that the fact not only angered him but surprised him too. "That being so, I will leave you to your prying, *mademoiselle*!"

"Oh, but – " He turned his head and she met the steel grey eyes head on, her fingers curling tightly into her palms. "I've told you, I don't intend doing anything worse than take a walk," she said, and he eyed her narrowly for a moment, then he eased his broad shoulders into the merest suggestion of a shrug.

"*Très bien, mademoiselle*," he said, but with very little conviction, and let in the clutch.

The big car moved off smoothly down the village street and Jesamine watched it go, wondering how on earth she had allowed herself to be influenced. It was a journalist's job to find out things, hurtful or not, but somehow she simply could not bring herself to do anything that was likely to prove hurtful to Paul d'Armor, and admitting that, even to herself, was oddly disturbing.

Grosvallée was not an outstandingly pretty village in a province that abounded with pretty villages, but it had a quiet charm that mellowed in the warm sun and its huddle of narrow houses pushed their steep sloping roofs up through the surrounding plane trees lining both sides of the street and the square.

There were a couple of small shops, including a tiny *boulangerie* whose delicious smells drifted towards her on the light wind, and the inevitable café, although this was not the kind so beloved of tourists. There were no colourful umbrellas here, set out over small tables, but a couple of rough benches and wooden trestles where the old men of the village passed their days, taking their ease and imbibing the local wines in their less vintage forms.

A little church, built from the local granite, stood back from the street amid a veritable forest of plane trees whose leaves sprinkled broken sunlight over its sombre walls like a scattering of golden coins. It was a short ungainly building that reflected the same homely, lopsided look that many Breton churches had, but its surroundings softened its inelegant design and the whole picture was peaceful and infinitely pleasing.

A stone Calvary, such a feature of Breton life, shared the church's shrouded privacy, crudely carved as so many of them were, but with a touching simplicity that suggested a child might have made the short squat crucifix and the stiff little figures surrounding it. One of the frequent *pardons*, Jesamine promised herself, was something she must try and see before she left Brittany.

There seemed fewer people about than when she had come the previous Sunday, for no doubt most of the men were at work, but she was still the target for several pairs of eyes as she stood for a moment in front of the little church, just beyond the barrier of trees that surrounded it.

Several old men sitting on a bench against the wall of the café kept their narrow-eyed gaze on her while they smoked and sipped their wine, so also did the two elderly women who chatted together in the doorway of the little *boulangerie* with warm new bread hugged to their breasts. Of course, they had seen Paul d'Armor let her out of his car. They had probably witnessed that seductive attempt of his to change her mind about visiting the village, and speculation was rife. It was only to be expected in a place as small as Grosvallée.

She was unaware that there was anyone nearer at hand until a quiet voice murmured words of apology in French from immediately behind her, and she turned swiftly, startled out of her reverie. An elderly priest stood at her elbow, his gaze every bit as curious as the old men and the women in the *boulangerie,* and she wondered if he too had seen her arrival.

He indicated with an explanatory wave of his hand that she was standing right in front of the gate to the church and blocking his way. Hastily she stepped aside, smiling apologetically. "Oh, I'm sorry, Father," she said. "I didn't realise I was in your way."

"*Mais non, mademoiselle,*" the old priest assured her, "you have no need to apologise. You wished to speak with me, perhaps? I am Père Dominic, *mademoiselle,* if I may assist you?"

"I'm not sure if you can," Jesamine confessed, and laughed a little uncertainly. She had told Paul d'Armor that she was concerned only with information to do with Charles Louis Vernais, but perhaps the priest might know something of him, of where he was buried for instance. "To be perfectly honest," she told him, "I was miles away when you surprised me, Father!"

The old priest looked puzzled. "*Comment, mademoiselle?*"

Jesamine hastened to explain. "I was thinking about something quite different," she told him. "My mind was wandering, Father, that's what I meant. I've quite a lot on my mind at the moment."

"Ah!" He nodded understanding. "You are troubled, *mon enfant?*" His bright curious eyes were frankly speculating and she knew without doubt that he had seen her with Paul d'Armor. "If it is a spiritual problem, then be assured, *mademoiselle,* I can help you!"

Jesamine shook her head, though she smiled her appreciation of his intentions. "Oh no, Father, thank you," she told him, "it's nothing like that."

"*Non?*" He seemed in no hurry to go, and she wondered if he altogether believed her. "Mademoiselle is English?"

he guessed, and smiled when she confirmed it. "We do not have the tourist in Grosvallée so often, *mademoiselle*, you are most welcome!"

"Thank you, but I'm not a tourist, Father," she explained. "In fact I'm here to work – I'm staying at the Château d'Armor."

Sparse grey brows fluttered swiftly into a grizzled forelock and the old priest eyed her with even more curiosity. "Mademoiselle is employed at the château?" he asked, and made no secret of the fact that he found it hard to believe.

"Oh no," Jesamine told him with a smile, "I don't actually work *for* the d'Armor family. I'm a journalist and they're very kindly putting me up as well as helping me with my story."

Père Dominic looked stunned for several seconds, then he shook his head. "You write of the *famille* d'Armor?" he asked. "I find that very hard to believe, *mademoiselle*!" He shook his head hastily as if to recall his last impulsive words and shrugged his shoulders with an eloquence characteristic of so many of his race. "Things change, *naturellement*," he said with an air of resignation, and shook his head.

Jesamine looked at him curiously, her interest plain in her eyes. "You seem surprised, *monsieur*," she said, and again the old man shrugged.

"One sees many changes, *mademoiselle*," he said noncommittally.

She looked past him at the squat little church, gold flecked in the summer sunshine and sought a more agreeable subject, as she thought. "Like your old church," she said with a smile. "I'd like to see it, if I may, Father, it must have seen some dramatic changes in its time. Even during the past forty years or so, I suppose. This village was occupied during the last war, wasn't it?"

He did not answer immediately and Jesamine thought her question troubled him, although heaven knew why, and he was looking at her thoughtfully, almost in the way that Paul had – as if he suspected her motives. "For a while, *mademoiselle*," he said quietly.

"You were here?" she asked, and he shrugged, that eloquent response to so many questions. "It must have been hard for you," she suggested. "For everyone, of course, but for a priest particularly so, I imagine."

"War is hard on everyone, *mademoiselle*," he observed.

"Yes, of course." She smiled and pulled a rueful face, as if apologising for her lack of years. "I'm too young to have been born then, of course," she said.

"*Naturellement!*"

Her next observation was inevitable, when she thought about it, and she really meant nothing significant by it, despite the priest's rather dramatic reaction. "The d'Armors were here too, of course," she said. "They must have been involved in some way, I'm sure – I can't believe they weren't!"

They had walked part way along the overgrown path to the church, but Père Dominic came to a stop suddenly and looked at her narrowly. "*Mademoiselle*," he said firmly but quietly, "the *famille* d'Armor have always been held in respect in Grosvallée, it is not my place to discuss their private affairs with a *journaliste*!"

Jesamine stared at him for a second, surprised by the vehemence of his objection, then she shook her head slowly and sought to remedy the impression she had apparently given him – that she was there to pry into the affairs of the d'Armor family. The same worry that Paul seemed to have and which now puzzled her more than ever.

"Oh, but you're wrong, Father," she said anxiously. "I –"

"I think you have curiosity about the daughter of the family whose guest you are, *mademoiselle*, and I cannot allow myself to be your informant!"

"Louise d'Armor?" Jesamine's heart was thudding at her ribs suddenly and she looked at the old priest for several seconds before it occurred to her to deny the charge he made against her. It was possible, more, it was likely, that he had been her confessor. He would know more about her mystery than anyone else. "But, Father," she said, "I know nothing about Louise d'Armor, she hasn't even been mentioned."

"*Précisément!*" Père Dominic said firmly. "So you come seeking the information you require elsewhere! I am discouraged, *mademoiselle* – I had misjudged you!"

"You're misjudging me now, Father!" she insisted earnestly. "I didn't come here to ask about Louise d'Armor – I simply mentioned that the family must have been here during the war. I promised Paul, Monsieur Paul d'Armor, that I wouldn't pry into anything else, and I haven't!"

For several moments the old priest said nothing, his grey head was bowed and he seemed to have left her, in spirit if not in body. Then he raised his head suddenly and there was a hint of a smile on his weathered face as he looked at her. "Forgive me, *mademoiselle*," he said, "I was perhaps too hasty in my judgment. Time has healed many things, but it is still too easy to – suspect!"

"Of course!" She had no idea what he was referring to and it was unthinkable that she could even allude to the existence of Louise d'Armor now, much as she would have liked to. "In fact, Father," she told him, "I'm here to write a history of a mutual ancestor I share with the d'Armors – Charles Louis Vernais, the last Comte d'Armor."

"Ah, *mais oui!*" His relief was obvious. "It is to discover history that you are here, *mademoiselle*! Your own ancestor also, you say?"

"That's right," Jesamine agreed, thankful to be back on good terms. "Monsieur and Madame d'Armor have been very helpful but I wondered, Father, if there was anything more you could tell me about him. Perhaps if I could see where he's buried."

The old man was interested in her task, that was evident, but he was shaking his head regretfully over her last request. "*Non, mon enfant,*" he told her gently. "The *famille* d'Armor have their own private chapel in the grounds of the château, they are buried there – I also am *curé* there."

"Oh!" The news stunned her for a moment, and she sifted through all the information the d'Armor family had given her regarding Charles Louis Vernais. Not once had they mentioned the existence of a private chapel in the château grounds. "Thank you, Father!" She smiled at the old priest, knowing he did not realise that he had, for all his caution, told her something about his *patrons* that she did not know before.

She took leave of Père Dominic and started to walk back to the Château d'Armor, even though she had spoken to no one else. There was a great deal on her mind as she walked back along the vine-bordered road, not least the reason why no one had told her of the existence of the private chapel where Charles Louis was buried.

CHAPTER FOUR

THERE was little use pretending she had any reason to stay any longer at the Château d'Armor, although Jesamine would have liked to think there was. In the four full days she had already been there she had accumulated as much data as she could possibly use in one article, and last night she had spent quite a long time typing it out on her portable.

James still had to take his photographs, of course, but he would be arriving from Nantes in a few hours and after that she could not possibly claim she needed more time. The whole thing was finished, packed into an envelope in her handbag and ready to post.

It was a fine bright morning and that made it even harder to leave, for the view from her bedroom window looked so enchanting in the morning sunlight. Louise Sutton, from her place in the alcove, looked out with her innocent eyes and filled her with a curious restlessness, a desire to know more about the family who had housed her for so long without even knowing who she was. But it was no use, her reason for being there was finished, and she had no alternative but to go home.

Downstairs in the white-walled breakfast room she found herself in the company of Paul d'Armor and his grandfather.

Madame d'Armor was not yet up and somehow Jesamine missed her this morning, for she felt oddly vulnerable in the company of the two men with the prospect before her of telling them she was leaving.

François d'Armor, a prisoner in his chair as always, looked remarkably fresh for first thing in the morning, but she had very soon come to the conclusion that the old man had a remarkably resilient spirit, despite his physical handicap. She was a little startled to realise that she would actually miss him quite a lot, and especially his fund of historical tales which he told with such verve and panache.

Paul sat facing her, in his usual position at the table, and she tried hard not to notice things about him that she found so incredibly disturbing to her self-control. Small, seemingly unimportant things that she always noticed about him and wished she did not. For one thing, the way his muscular brown arms were revealed by the rolled-up sleeves of a blue denim shirt, and his throat and the first few inches of broad chest that were visible in the open neck.

He had said little to her as yet, nothing beyond a brief good morning, but she was no less physically aware of him, and she consoled herself with the fact that it was probably as well she was leaving, before she fell in love with him.

There were any number of reasons why she would like to have stayed longer at the château. There was the mystery of Louise d'Armor, for one thing, and the curious reticence and suspicion of the old priest in the village. Then there was the complete silence of an otherwise garrulous old man on the subject of his only child – a series of intriguing, half-learned things that aroused her journalistic curiosity and which were unlikely to be explained now.

Most of all, though, she was reluctant to say goodbye to Paul d'Armor. If she allowed herself to fall in love with him it was almost certain he would cause her much the same kind of heartache that Louise Sutton had known, but still she wanted to know him better. It remained to be seen what his reaction would be to her going.

"I shan't like leaving," she said as she poured herself

coffee, "I've enjoyed myself so much; but I must go tomorrow."

She was uncertain whether or not Paul looked up when she said it, although after their conversation yesterday he must feel some surprise. She had implied then that she was prepared to take rooms in the village if he made it impossible for her to stay on at the château, and at the time she had meant every word. It was only after a phone call from James last night, telling her of his imminent arrival, that she had realised there would be no valid reason for her to stay on after today, and she had decided to break the news to her host this morning at breakfast.

It was evident how old François d'Armor felt, for his bright old eyes expressed frank disappointment. "You mean to leave us so soon, *mademoiselle*?" he asked, and Jesamine smiled ruefully.

"I'm afraid so, Monsieur d'Armor," she said. "I should have told you sooner instead of springing it on you so abruptly this morning, but – well, quite frankly I didn't realise until last night after James rang that there's no reason for me to stay any longer. I have the article here all ready to post, and James should be here some time this morning to take the photographs."

"Ah! Your friend is recovered?"

She nodded and smiled. "Yes, thank heaven. He rang last night, rather late, to say that he'd left hospital and he'll be here this morning. It won't take him very long to take the pictures we need, and after that –"

She shrugged and for the first time realised that as a means of conveying inexpressible meanings, the Gallic shrug was unsurpassable. It must have conveyed exactly how she felt too, for François d'Armor was watching her closely, with shrewd dark eyes.

"But you do not wish to leave?" he guessed.

The swift glance she gave in Paul's direction was more instinctive than deliberate, but his grandfather did not fail to notice that either, and Jesamine saw his eyes narrow suddenly, as if in speculation. "I've enjoyed being here," she admitted without hesitation. "I've really enjoyed it more than anything else I've done, because for one thing I've never worked in such marvellous surroundings before."

"Also you discover your ancestor, *la belle* Louise," he reminded her, and Jesamine smiled.

"That was a wonderful and unexpected bonus," she said. "I never thought I'd actually see what she looked like and then suddenly – you produce a picture of her and give a whole new dimension to her story!"

"There can be no mistake that it is Mademoiselle Sutton, eh?" he asked with a smile. "She is – *très belle*, like her – many times granddaughter!"

"It was very observant of Madame d'Armor to spot the likeness," Jesamine said. "I can still hardly believe it!"

"But there is no mistake, *mon enfant*," he assured her. "None at all, eh, Paul?"

Having his opinion sought, Paul looked up from buttering a roll and studied her face for a moment with those steady grey eyes. "None at all," he agreed after a moment or two, and Jesamine determinedly kept her own eyes averted.

"The face of an angel, *n'est-ce pas?*" the old man persisted, and Paul took a moment or two to answer. When he did it was in French and too soft-voiced for her to have caught the words properly, even had she been able to understand them.

"That is where we differ, I'm afraid," she said, and laughed in a way that sounded oddly defensive. "I lay no claim to being an angel!"

"*Mais non*," old François said, "and neither was your ancestor, *ma chère!*" He reached across and squeezed her fingers. "No matter, *mademoiselle*, we have enjoyed your company, angel or no, and I am reluctant to see you go!"

"You've been very generous and helpful, Monsieur d'Armor." She smiled at him, her glance flicking only briefly in Paul's direction. "I'm very grateful to you for all you've done, but it *is* possible to overstay one's welcome and I'll have absolutely no excuse, once James has taken his pictures, to stay any longer." She laughed and was startled to realise how forced it sounded. "I have to admit," she said, "that I've taken much longer over this assignment than I usually do – thanks to your wonderful hospitality."

He leaned forward again across the table and once more his bony fingers enclosed her hand, his smile friendly and persuasive. "Then will you not stay on and enjoy more of our hospitality, *mon enfant*?" he asked, and squeezed her fingers gently. "You are a free agent, are you not? You have the time to stay with us for longer if you wish?"

"Oh yes, I have the time," Jesamine agreed, almost too stunned by the invitation to think clearly. She would have given much to know what Paul d'Armor was thinking, but he had not even looked up as far as she could tell, though she could guess he would not view his grandfather's impulsive gesture with much enthusiasm.

"Also, are you not family?" the old man said, pressing on with the plea.

It was difficult not to look across at Paul, but she managed it and shook her head to deny her right to claim kinship. "I can't really claim to belong to your family, Monsieur d'Armor," she told him.

"Ah! A mere matter of a few generations!" old François insisted with a sweeping gesture of his hand. "Why should we not extend a welcome to you when you are so much the image of our *fille de la nuit*? Charles Louis Vernais, I am sure, would rise from his grave to reproach us if we did not persuade you to stay when you are so much the image of his *belle* Louise!"

The offer was tempting, there was no denying it, but Jesamine was aware from the corner of her eye that Paul was taking an interest at last, and watching her closely. The glint in his eyes could even have been a warning, she could not tell, and she hesitated. "I – I'm not sure if I should, Monsieur d'Armor," she told the old man "It seems rather an imposition after you've been so helpful, to inflict myself on you for even longer. You must surely be anxious to have your home to yourselves again."

"But how can such charming company grow tedious?" François d'Armor demanded, and Jesamine flicked a brief, curious glance in Paul's direction.

"Perhaps," she ventured, "Monsieur Paul –"

"Paul would be delighted, *naturellement*," she was assured. His dark eyes glowed wickedly from below his sparse white brows and seemed to give lie to those eighty-eight years he claimed. "Also I would delight in your company, *ma chère*," he told her, "for you listen without complaint to my *histoire*!"

"That's because I enjoy listening," Jesamine said with a smile. "My own grandfather's a wonderful story-teller, and you have the same gift."

"Then, *chère mademoiselle*," he said, squeezing her fingers, "*encouragez moi, s'il vous plaît!*"

She was weakening, Jesamine thought, as she had known she would, and there was no real reason why she should not accept the invitation. After all, François d'Armor was still the nominal head of his household – but she wished Paul would do something more positive than sit there silently eating his breakfast, as if he had little or no interest in the matter.

He could not pretend it did not affect him, for he had expressed his opinion far too forcibly for her to believe that was so, but if only he would say something. She looked across at him from the concealment of her lashes and was startled to find herself looking straight into those cool, challenging eyes.

"It is possible that Mademoiselle is considering something I have said to her, Grandpère," he suggested quietly, and his grandfather frowned curiously.

"*Comment?*"

A smile touched Paul's mouth and gleamed in the depths of his grey eyes, so that Jesamine hastily looked away. "I had reason to suspect that Mademoiselle Arden was becoming too curious about matters that do not concern her," he explained frankly, "and I informed her that, should that prove so, I would have no hesitation in – throwing her out. Is that not the phrase, *mademoiselle?*"

Jesamine flushed. She was not easily flustered, but Paul d'Armor seemed to possess the ability to find her weak spots with disconcerting ease, and it made her feel horribly vulnerable. "That's the phrase, *monsieur*," she agreed, determinedly steadying her voice.

"*Mon dieu!*" the old man said with surprising force. "I cannot believe it!"

"But you can see why I hesitate to accept your invitation, Monsieur d'Armor," Jesamine said. "I wouldn't want to stay if Monsieur Paul suspects me of prying into – secrets."

"There are no secrets, *mademoiselle!*" the old man stated firmly, and once more looked at his grandson as if he considered he had taken leave of his senses. "Have you no *galanterie, mon cher* Paul?"

"None!" Paul declared flatly, and his eyes gleamed like grey steel. "Mademoiselle Arden will tell you so, Grandpère!"

"Then I will ask her pardon!" the old man retorted sharply, and turned once more to Jesamine. "Mademoiselle Arden!" he appealed, "must I be deprived of your company by my grandson's *inhospitalité?* For a short time at least, will you not remain with us, *s'il vous plaît?*"

With her own inclinations very much in favour of accepting, Jesamine found it hard to refuse, even though Paul's attitude left her in little doubt how he felt about the idea. There was also Madame d'Armor, whose opinion had not yet been sought. It was quite possible that she would share her grandson's view, in fact Jesamine would be surprised if she did not.

She had proved a pleasant enough hostess, once her initial suspicions had been lulled, but a prolonged stay was a different matter from the few days she was expecting to have a stranger under her roof. In the meantime, François d'Armor was pressing for an answer. "*Mademoiselle?*" he prompted, and Jesamine, ever a creature of impulse, glanced briefly again at Paul d'Armor, then nodded.

If Paul objected then she would have to deal with his objections if and when they arose, but the thought of staying on, for however long, offered an exciting prospect she could not resist. "Thank you, Monsieur d'Armor," she said. "I'd love to stay, if you're quite sure I shan't be —"

"You will be welcome to stay as long as you wish," François informed her, and looked at his grandson with a suggestion of the same haughty challenge that Paul himself so often expressed. "I cannot believe that my sentiments do not equally apply to my grandson," he said, "but if he dislikes the idea of a lovely girl staying in his home, then he is not the man I have always believed him to be!"

Paul said nothing for a moment, but there was a curious expression on his face when he glanced across at Jesamine and he murmured something in French to his grandfather. Whatever it was was unintelligible to Jesamine, but the old man seemed to find it amusing, for he laughed and shook his head, his bright dark eyes twinkling at his grandson.

Puzzled, Jesamine glanced from one to the other and, after a few seconds François d'Armor leaned across and patted her hand reassuringly. "Your pardon, *cher enfant*," he begged, "it is unforgivable that we speak so when you do not understand our language." He shook his head, still smiling. "But this was – how do you say? – an exchange between men, not to be repeated to a lady, though not *grossier* as you might suppose. It is simply that we know one another too well, my grandson and I, better than I had realised, it seems. You will forgive us, *cher mademoiselle?*"

Jesamine would have given much to know exactly what it was that Paul d'Armor had said to his grandfather. She did not for one minute believe it had been a family joke at all, but she would hate to see the old man embarrassed by his grandson's probably earthy comment, so she passed it off in the easiest way she knew.

"Oh please, don't apologise," she said, "I don't mind in the least, *monsieur*. Every family has its own private jokes – we do at home. I'm not offended!"

"You are very understanding, *mademoiselle!*" His thin shoulders shrugged, expressing heaven knew what implication, but his eyes were kind and friendly, and once more Jesamine warmed to the man behind the smile. "I hope you will also understand that it would give me great pleasure to have you stay as our guest for a while longer."

Her eyes strayed instinctively to Paul, and she met the

70

cool look he gave her as steadily as she could. "Thank you, *monsieur*," she said, and wondered if Paul would at last make some comment in English.

Instead he drank down the last of his coffee, then got up from the table with a murmured excuse and Jesamine's eyes followed his tall striding figure to the door. Turning in the doorway he looked back and the steady grey eyes held an expression that was by now all too familiar to her. Laughter, mockery and that disturbing hint of challenge.

"Enjoy your stay, *mademoiselle*," he said, and closed the door firmly behind him.

Whether or not Madame d'Armor had been told of her proposed holiday, Jesamine had little time to discover that morning, for James Terril arrived before lunch, for the overdue photographic session, and she was kept busy helping him, deciding which shots were best to illustrate what she had written.

She had foreseen no opposition from James when she told him she would be staying on for a couple of weeks more, and she was a little surprised when he objected quite strongly. He looked pale still, but he seemed to have recovered well from the virus that had laid him low, and she had to admit to being glad to see him again.

She had worked with James quite a bit and they got on very well together, but she had never known him take a really personal interest in her affairs, certainly not to the extent of remarking that he thought she was making a mistake in staying on at the Château d'Armor. They were walking together in the gardens just after lunch when she told him about her decision to have a holiday, and he had at once frowned at her disapprovingly.

He had a cheerful and rather boyishly good-looking face normally, but at the moment his brows were drawn into a frown above light blue eyes that expressed his dislike of the idea, and she found his reaction rather puzzling. "I suppose it's got something to do with that sexy Frenchman, hasn't it, Jess?" he asked bluntly, and Jesamine wished there was something she could do about the unexpected flush of colour that warmed her cheeks.

She had not expected that kind of remark from James, and she wondered why he should suddenly start taking an interest in her private life. "Paul d'Armor?" she asked, as casually as she knew how. "Oh, for heaven's sake, James, you can't be serious – not about *him*!"

James thrust his hands deep into the pockets of his slacks and gave her a sideways glance that questioned both her tone and her attitude. "Are you going to tell me that you don't find him attractive?" he asked, and it was obvious that he would not believe it if she did.

"Of course I find him attractive," Jesamine admitted without hesitation. "He's a very attractive man – sexy, as you say, but he hasn't time for me I can assure you, and as for me – I'm far more inclined to have murderous thoughts about him than romantic ones! He can be so – so condescending and autocratic, you've no idea!"

"I've a very *good* idea," James remarked dryly, "but I've known women who find an arrogant devil like that irresistible. From what I saw of him at lunch, I'd say Monsieur Paul d'Armor is a highly dangerous package to have in close proximity to a young girl!"

Jesamine laughed a little shakily. Jealousy was a new facet of James's character, but she was ready to swear it was jealousy that gave rise to those caustic observations on Paul d'Armor. Also it was likely that his opinion would in time be relayed to her family in England, and she was anxious that they should not be given any wrong impression of her unscheduled holiday.

"I'm not a young girl, James," she told him. "I'm as near twenty-five as no matter —"

"You're only twenty-four," James interrupted flatly.

"But I'm not a sheltered little home girl," Jesamine insisted. "I'm quite capable of taking care of myself, James — if I need to."

"You'll need to," James prophesied, "and you're used to having me around to look out for you, Jess, you're not the independent little hardcase you like to think you are — I know you!"

"Not as well as you think you do, evidently," Jesamine declared, although she was uncertain just how seriously to take his estimation of her. She had been around quite a lot during her brief but successful journalistic career, but never alone, and she had never before come into contact with anyone quite like Paul d'Armor.

"Just the same," James insisted firmly, "if you're going to stay on here I'd better take a room somewhere nearby, just to keep an eye on you."

"Oh no, James, you can't!" She looked at him wide-eyed, imagining the repercussions that could have. "Please, I don't need anyone to look after me, and if you stay around it will look as if — the d'Armors will think —"

"That I'm looking out for you," James finished for her, "and they'll be right. I'm not going home and leaving you here in the same house as that predatory Frenchman, Jess, I don't trust him!"

"Then trust me!" said Jesamine, and looked at him appealingly. His opinion of Paul d'Armor merely confirmed her own, but it was much more discomfiting somehow, hearing it expressed by someone else, and she looked away hastily for fear he read the doubt in her eyes.

"I do trust you, love," James assured her, "but him — I wouldn't trust him within a mile of any female I cared twopence about. He's dangerous, and I mean to see you don't come to any harm!"

"*No*, James!" She stood her ground firmly, determined not to be coddled as James intended. "I don't need a chaperone, I really don't, and I'd hate – well, I'd hate Paul d'Armor to realise you were keeping an eye on me."

"You think it'd cramp his style?" James asked.

"It wouldn't do anything except amuse him!" Jesamine told him shortly. "And I won't have him laughing at me because you so obviously think he – has designs on me! If you think I'm going to give him the satisfaction of taunting me with your over-protective fear for my reputation, you're very much mistaken! I'd much rather you went home and left me to enjoy my holiday!"

James shook his head. "Not a chance, love. I agree it probably wouldn't cramp his style at all, but at least I'll be around if you yell for help."

They had come into the gardens ostensibly to say their goodbyes before James left for home, but Jesamine knew he would put off his departure indefinitely, if he thought she had the slightest need for him. It was touching to be the object of such loyalty and devotion, but the thought of Paul d'Armor realising his motive for staying and laughing at her for it made her curl up inside.

James brought them to a halt beside one of the big chestnut trees that surrounded the château. Leaning back against its rough trunk, he turned her to face him and there was a deep, anxious look in his eyes that dismissed all previous efforts to treat the matter lightly. "Jess, listen to me," he pleaded. "I recognise Paul d'Armor's type, more easily than you do, apparently. He's the sort who leaves a trail of ex-lovers all over the countryside and never feels a twinge himself. He's a heartbreaker, Jess, and if you stay on here alone, you could get hurt, I know it – you can't touch a man like that."

She laughed a little unsteadily and was not at all sure that she was telling the truth, only anxious to convince herself as well as James. "I'm not his type, James," she told him. "You don't have to worry!"

His laugh was short and harsh. "You're a woman, aren't you?" he asked dryly, then raised her chin with one gentle hand and looked down at her for a moment, shaking his head. "You *could* fall in love with him, couldn't you, my sweet?" he asked, and Jesamine took a moment to admit it.

"Maybe I could if I let myself," she admitted slowly, "but not if I'm on my guard, and I shan't be as easily swept off my feet as you seem to expect, James."

He regarded her steadily for a moment or two, then, apparently realising how resolved she was, he sighed and shook his head. "O.K., love, there's nothing I can do, I suppose," he said resignedly, "except be around to pick up the pieces." He bent his head and kissed her mouth – a light gentle kiss that stirred no erotic reactions in her, but touched her emotions in quite another way.

"You're the nicest man I know, James," she told him in a soft, husky voice, and tiptoed to return the kiss, "but I really *don't* need you as a bodyguard. I can cope with Paul d'Armor, I promise you." She smiled at him confidently, as if she was firmly convinced of what she said, and only in her innermost heart did she admit she might be wrong.

James left, though with obvious reluctance, not long after lunch, but for all his assurances Jesamine suspected he would find some excuse before very long to fly back to France. He had not been at all happy about going and James was immovable once he had something fixed in his head.

He did not trust Paul and sooner or later, she felt certain he would turn up again on some pretext or other. In the meantime, she thought, François d'Armor was speculating about her relationship with James, and she was quite prepared for a few searching questions on the subject.

It was a relief when Madame d'Armor showed no sign of being openly against her prolonged stay, although Jesamine had the feeling that she would have been happier to see her leave when James did. Paul gave the impression that he was resigned to the inevitable, but did not necessarily like it, and she wondered if he really would have found James' fears for her amusing.

Once James was gone, Jesamine was left with a curiously lost feeling that she could only attribute to all those dire warnings that he had issued regarding Paul, a feeling she shook off impatiently. Nothing had really changed, except that she was now purely and simply a guest at the château instead of a journalist doing a job, but somehow even that minor change made her feel differently, and she wondered if she had done the right thing in staying after all.

She put on her favourite dress to go down to dinner that evening because she felt in need of a boost for her morale and she knew how much the deep rose pink suited her dark hair and creamy skin. It was a very feminine dress too, and could not fail to win the approval of her host, at least.

Its soft neckline flattered the smoothness of her neck and shoulders and the bodice clung lovingly to the gentle curves beneath it, and when she walked into the big, brightly lit dining salon Paul's eyes sought her immediately. Once more James's warnings came into her mind, making her more than usually self conscious, when he raised one fair brow as if in comment and half-smiled. He swept his eyes in one long, calculating look over her from head to toe, a look that James would have recognised and resented, but Jesamine felt no resentment, only a curious tingling sensation along her spine as she briefly met his eyes before walking over to take her place at the table.

Monsieur and Madame d'Armor were already seated and Paul pulled out her chair for her with smooth practised movements that managed somehow to bring his hard brown hands into contact with the softness of her shoulders, so that she glanced only briefly over her shoulder when she thanked him.

Bending forward to push in her chair for her brought him much too close for comfort and the warmth of his body with its suggestion of restrained power, mingled with some spicy masculine scent, set her pulses racing. She almost held her breath until he walked round and took his own seat opposite, and once sitting there she had no option but to be constantly aware of him for the rest of the meal.

She had been right about François d'Armor approving of the rose pink dress, and she guessed that the old man must have been something of a gallant in his day. There was a glow in his bright dark eyes as he leaned across the corner of the table towards her and smiled. "*La rose anglaise,*" he murmured. "You look – *très charmante, ma chère*!"

Jesamine felt quite lighthearted suddenly, and she smiled at him with a hint of mischief in her eyes. "Thank you, Monsieur d'Armor," she told him. "You're very good for my morale!"

"You have the need of a – lift for the morale?" the old man asked, as if it was beyond belief. "Surely not, *mademoiselle*!"

Jesamine smiled and shook her head. "Oh, I can assure you my morale is often in need of a boost," she told him, and he looked at her for a moment with bright curious eyes.

"You are perhaps missing the company of Monsieur

Terril, your friend?" he suggested, and Jesamine could have laughed aloud at the accuracy of her guess that he would mention it sooner or later. The surprise was that it was so soon and so openly.

Madame d'Armor, however, was shaking her head and looking at her husband reproachfully. "François," she scolded him, "such questions will embarrass Mademoiselle Arden!"

"Oh no, it's quite all right," Jesamine hastened to assure her. "I don't mind talking about James, Madame d'Armor." She turned back to the old man and smiled. "I'm used to working with James," she told him, "but he was ill, so there was nothing I could do but wait for him to join me. It's a pity he missed having the few days here with me, but he's always very busy and unlike me he can't take a holiday at the moment."

François d'Armor would not leave it there, she should have known, and he was still eyeing her with that bright, knowing glint in his eyes. "You know him very well?" he ventured, and Jesamine nodded agreement.

"Pretty well, I suppose," she agreed, and laughed. "Although James claims to know *me* better than I know myself!"

His white head nodding, François d'Armor tapped the side of his nose with a forefinger, obviously putting his own construction on that. "Ah!" he said. "An *affaire de coeur, n'est-ce pas?*"

Once more Madame d'Armor looked at him reproachfully, but this time she said nothing, and again Jesamine shook her head to deny the implication he made. It was purely instinctive when she looked at Paul from the concealment of her lashes, remembering his lecture to her on the matter of *affaires de coeur*, while they stood in the hall in front of Charles Louis Vernais's portrait. She recalled too, her own suggestion that he spoke from experience, and his confirmation of her suspicions.

"A love affair?" She smiled at the old man, trying to put James in Paul d'Armor's position and unable to do so. "Oh no, Monsieur d'Armor, there's nothing like that with James and me. He's a friend, a very good friend, and a working colleague, that's all."

"So?" She was unsure whether or not he believed her, but Paul was watching her from the other side of the table.

"Consider, Grandpère," he said in a quiet matter-of-fact voice, "if such an affair existed would Mademoiselle Arden have taken such pains to persuade Monsieur Terril to leave without her?" His eyes held hers steadily and that hint of challenge lingered again in his gaze. "You *did* make quite an effort to persuade him to go without you, did you not, *mademoiselle*?" he asked, soft-voiced, and Jesamine curled her hands tightly and quite involuntarily.

"I saw no reason for James to stay on," she told him, without even stopping to wonder how he came to be so well informed. "It was silly for him to – "

"But he did not wish to go and leave you, *n'est-ce pas*?" Paul insisted, and she hesitated for a moment before she answered him.

"He – he would rather have stayed," she admitted, and was aware that both Monsieur and Madame d'Armor were looking at her curiously.

Paul's eyes glinted like grey steel and she knew he was laughing at her. Her hands curled even more tightly as she fought a desire to be angrily rude to him and her blue eyes matched his for brightness as she looked at him with her chin lifted. "As your – *protecteur*?" he suggested, and it seemed to Jesamine obvious that he knew well enough who and what it was that James had wanted to protect her from.

"James is naturally protective about females," she said,

controlling her voice with an effort. "He usually travels with me and takes care of everything." She laughed a little uncertainly and was careful to avoid looking at Paul again. "He thinks I'm incapable of looking after myself in a strange country, although I've managed perfectly well the past few days without him."

"He is concerned for you, *naturellement*," François d'Armor said, nodding his head, as if he understood James's motives perfectly. "It is to be expected when a man is – perhaps just a little in love with his lovely companion, *n'est-ce pas*?"

Jesamine laughed. It was useless trying to convince him that James was anything other than in love with her, but she was becoming a little concerned with the fact that her emotional situation was the hub of the conversation. "Neither James or I are in love as far as I know, Monsieur d'Armor," she told him firmly. "We've worked together for some time now, but there's never been any suggestion of anything – we *are* just friends, that's all."

"So!" His shrug suggested he was still to be convinced, but would refrain from voicing his doubts for the sake of politeness. "You surprise me, *ma chère!* Let us hope that our own young men will prove less disappointing in the cause of *l'amour*, hmm?"

His meaning was obvious enough for Jesamine to glance swiftly and instinctively at Paul, directly opposite, and she was appalled to find herself looking straight into those steely grey eyes that mocked her with laughter. "Oh, I'm not too concerned about that, Monsieur d'Armor," she assured the old man breathlessly, and hastily looked away again. "I don't have much time for – *l'amour* when I'm working!"

"But you are not now working, *mon enfant*," the old man reminded her gently, and she instinctively followed the direction of his gaze again, without realising what she was doing.

She felt a strange curling sensation in her stomach when she saw the smile on Paul's mouth and again met the mockery in his eyes. Perhaps she had been too rash after all and should at least have let James stay within call. That look of Paul d'Armor's was infinitely disturbing, and she despaired of her own weakness.

CHAPTER FIVE

THE first two weeks of her holiday had passed so quickly that Jesamine found it hard to believe it could have been so long. François d'Armor was an excellent host and seemed genuinely to enjoy her company. He was, as she had remarked, a gifted *raconteur*, and she spent a considerable part of her time with him during those two weeks, listening to his stories or looking at the treasures he seemed to lay so little store by.

Both Jesamine's parents were in the antique business, so that she had a fair idea of the value of the many beautiful things she was shown, and she wondered if her hosts had. Neither Monsieur nor Madame d'Armor seemed to realise just how much wealth, in the form of *objets d'art*, they had under their roof.

Old François confessed one day to having no idea exactly what there was, and certainly not how great their value would be on present-day markets. It was an admission that appalled Jesamine when she recalled how carefully everything in her parents' stock was itemised and catalogued. The collection housed in the Château d'Armor must be worth many times that of her parents' business, and yet no one had any idea of its value or even, in some cases, of its existence, until it was brought to notice by a visitor like herself.

She had no difficulty at all finding common ground on which to meet her host, but it was rather more unexpected to find that she had a mutual interest in cooking with Madame d'Armor. It delighted her to think that there was some subject on which she could converse with the old lady at length without coming up against that unnerving barrier of difficult pauses that had hitherto marked their conversation.

She did not really expect to see much of Paul during week-days, and her assumption was proved correct. He was out of the house for most of the day, and often disappeared in the evenings as well. During her first week-end there he had driven off early on Saturday morning and not returned until Sunday evening, and when he came back Jesamine thought she noticed a certain air of tension.

It was nothing specific, but as well as that suggestion of strain she noticed that neither of his grandparents asked him if he had enjoyed his week-end away, and the combination of circumstances led her to speculate on the reason. The most likely cause, she thought, was that he had spent the week-end with a woman friend of whom they did not approve. She had no proof that her speculation bore any resemblance to the truth, but it would come as no surprise if it had.

He was a virile and very attractively mature man, and it would hardly be surprising if he was to go off for an occasional week-end with one of his *paramours*. She had even suggested to him herself that he was no stranger to *affaires de coeur* and he had not denied it. What did surprise and dismay her was to discover how much she disliked the idea. His grandparents' concern was understandable, for as far as she knew, Paul was the sole heir to their considerable fortune and they must by now be concerning themselves about a wife and family for him, but her own concern was inexplicable and she did her best to dismiss it.

She had been at the château a little over two weeks, and she mused as she came downstairs one morning to breakfast that perhaps it was time she thought about going home.

She had set no time limit on her unexpected holiday, but it had already been generously long and she would hate to outstay her welcome.

There was a great deal she would miss when she left, more than she had found the first time, two weeks ago, when she had announced her intention of leaving. She felt quite unbelievably at home in the lovely old château and its beautiful gardens, and it was marvellous to have daily access to so many lovely and precious things, even though she still concerned herself with the haphazard precautions for their safety. Perhaps another week would not be thought too long. She would mention it at breakfast this morning, and perhaps leave next week-end.

The big hall was deserted as she came downstairs, and she paused, as she sometimes did, beside a favourite painting that hung on the staircase wall. She had noticed it first quite early on in her stay, while she was writing the story of Charles Louis Vernais, but she had little time then to spare for any other than the central subject of her story. Now it was possible for her to take a more leisurely interest and she found the subject of the other portrait, if anything, even more intriguing than Charles Louis himself.

The ever-knowledgeable Brigitte had informed her that the portrait depicted an earlier Comte d'Armor than Charles Louis, Raoul Amadis Vernais, and it had not taken her a long to decide that this particular gentleman bore an even closer resemblance to Paul d'Armor.

Dressed in the elegant flattery of dark green velvet and with his hair powdered, he looked out at her with the same bold, challenging look in his eyes, but his features were more rugged and earthy than those of Charles Louis and the likeness to Paul therefore even greater. Possibly owing to his hair being powdered, he looked more fair, but whatever the reason Jesamine found him irresistibly fascinating.

She should have remembered that the pair of light sandals she was wearing had heels that were not as firmly fixed as they might have been. They were pretty and she had chosen them because they flattered her slim feet and ankles, and she did not anticipate doing any walking that morning. But having put them on she had promptly forgotten about them or to make allowances for their insecure heels, and her forgetfulness proved her undoing.

She turned from the portrait of the green-coated gallant too suddenly for the unsteady heels to cope, and the heel of her left shoe gave way under her so suddenly that she felt a sensation of helplessness as she started to fall down the wide marble stairs. Her cry of surprise was brief and hardly audible, for she had barely time to realise what was happening, but her hands reached out wildly for something to cling to and save herself.

Instead of the white marble balustrade, however, her fingers encountered the smoothness of some woven material, something soft and yielding, that pulled apart in her hands to expose the solid warmth of a human body beneath it. She was not hurt, but she was brought up short and the breath knocked out of her when she collided with something only slightly less yielding than the cold marble, and a pair of strong arms held her close for a moment against a broad masculine chest.

Another second or two and she realised that the fabric she clung to so tightly was a blue denim shirt that in her desperate effort to save herself she had pulled open down the whole length of its front, scoring the tanned flesh beneath it with her nails. Angry red marks that looked as if they had been made by the claws of a cat.

"*Petite minette!*"

The voice would have identified the owner of the arms if nothing else had, and Jesamine felt her heart begin to thud wildly in her breast as she struggled to stand on her own feet. She looked up at Paul d'Armor, stunned for a few seconds, but hardly surprised to see laughter glittering in his eyes as he looked down at her, noting her flushed cheeks.

His hair, usually so tidily brushed, fell in a thick, disordered swathe across his forehead, as if his efforts to save her from a fall had been more hasty than studied, and the red scratches across his chest gave him a curiously savage look, so that she renewed her attempts to break the hold of his arms on her. He held her at arm's length, fully aware of her anxiety to stand alone, but refusing to release her until he saw fit.

"You should trim your claws, *petite minette*," he told her, and laughed softly when her eyes questioned the name he gave her. "Little pussy," he explained. "See how you scratched me when I caught you in my arms!"

"I'm sorry!" She felt alarmingly breathless and fought hard to control her trembling limbs. "I could feel myself falling," she explained, "and I – grabbed."

"I saw that you were falling, and I too – grabbed," he told her. His eyes still glittered with that disturbing laughter and added to her uneasiness, and she wished that, just for once, she could face him without feeling so horribly naïve.

"I'm glad you were there," she said. "I'd have gone all the way down the stairs if you hadn't been!"

"Almost certainly," he agreed calmly, "and you see what my reward is, *mademoiselle*!"

He indicated the scratches on his chest, but Jesamine spared only a brief glance, for there was something infinitely disturbing about that hard tanned body in such close proximity. He still held her, his large strong hands spanning her slim waist, and the warm palms through her thin dress suggested actual contact with her skin, so that she shivered.

"I've said I'm sorry!"

She was on the defensive and her retort was sharper than she perhaps intended, but it seemed impossible for her to react coolly towards him, especially in this sort of situation. Putting her hands over his, her fingers tingled at the touch of their tanned strength, but she managed to ease them from her waist, then stepped back carefully on the stair.

"You do not feel – *tremblante*?" he enquired, and Jesamine hastily shook her head without really knowing what he meant.

"I'm perfectly all right, thank you," she told him. "But you'd better get Brigitte to put something on those scratches in case they – "

"Pshaw!" He dismissed her concern with a careless hand. "I have been scratched before!"

"Oh!" She was not quite sure what to make of what seemed to her to be an extremely provocative remark. "Just the same," she insisted, "scratches can become infected."

His eyes glittered with amusement and he elevated one fair brow. "You think yourself so deadly, *mademoiselle*?" he asked.

Jesamine refused to be drawn into anything so blatantly provocative and she stepped to one side without answering, meaning to walk past him and return to her room. She could go nowhere until she had changed her shoes and she was anxious to leave his disturbing company as soon as possible.

"If you'll excuse me," she said in a voice that was dismayingly small and breathless, "I'll have to go and change my shoes. I can't wear these now the heel's broken."

"Neither can you safely walk upstairs in them," Paul informed her and, before she could do anything about it, he had lifted her into his arms and was carrying her back up the stairs.

"Put me down!"

Her hands pushed in vain at the broad chest and she could feel the warmth of colour that flooded into her cheeks. If someone should see them – and she thought particularly of Madame d'Armor, heaven knew what they would think. Things were certainly easier between her and the old lady lately, but she would surely view the present situation and its implications with suspicion.

Paul merely smiled; a small and rather ironic smile that recognised her fears and mocked her for them. "You do not weigh very much, *mademoiselle*," he remarked, and laughed, a soft, deep sound that rippled through both their bodies.

The grey eyes in the rugged brown face were much too close for comfort and she hastily avoided them as she put her hands again to his chest in an effort to make him put her down. "I can perfectly well walk, *monsieur*," she insisted. "Will you please let me stand on my own feet!"

There was a stunning excitement about being in his arms that alarmed her, and she could feel her heart beating so hard that it made her head spin. He had made no move to refasten the denim shirt and she was pressed close to the bold masculine warmth of his body as he carried her, so that she closed her eyes briefly, despairing of her own weakness.

First one sandal and then the other clattered on to the marble stairs as she made another effort to wriggle free of those inescapable arms, but to no avail. He did not put her down, only swore softly in French when she almost caused him to miss his footing on the stairs.

"*Zut!* Would you have us both with our necks broken, *petite idiote*?" he demanded.

The gallery was deserted – cool and shadowed with the morning sunshine that came in through the windows at either end and he dumped her unceremoniously on to her feet, then stood looking at her with a gleam of exasperation in his eyes, as if he resented her struggles to be free of him. Some form of thanks as due, she supposed, but it was difficult to know just what to say.

"Thank you, *monsieur*!"

She smoothed down her dress with hands that trembled like leaves, and she did not even try and look at him. She knew her face was flushed and that she stood even shorter beside him without her shoes, and she stood for a moment looking down at her bare feet on the dark red carpet with a curious sense of anticipation curling in her stomach.

She did not need to glance up to know that he was watching her, she could feel his gaze as unmistakably as if she met it directly, and she shivered inwardly at some unfamiliar excitement. "How long have you been with us now, *mademoiselle?*" he asked, and she was so surprised by the question that she looked up, swiftly and almost involuntarily.

The grey eyes were direct and steady, and she thought that disturbing glint of laughter still lurked there somewhere. "In all?" she said. "Almost exactly three weeks."

"So long?" An arched brow expressed surprise, although she was left in doubt whether he considered her stay already too long, or had not realised the time had passed so quickly.

"As a matter of fact," she said, once more studying her bare toes, "I thought I'd tell Monsieur d'Armor this morning that I'll make this the last week of my holiday, and go home next week-end. I've had two weeks' holiday, just over."

"You have no more time to spare?" he suggested. "Or is it that you tire of the quiet life, Mademoiselle Arden?"

It was a challenging question, but Jesamine refused to be drawn by it and simply gave him a straightforward answer. "I've enjoyed myself very much," she said, "but I think three weeks is quite long enough to impose on anyone's hospitality, however willing one's host is."

"And your host is willing, *mademoiselle!*" The tone of his voice was such that Jesamine ventured another upward glance. "Grandpère is not averse to the company of a lovely young girl," he assured her with a hint of cynicism. "Especially one who listens to his *histoire* with every appearance of enjoyment!"

"Oh, but I *do* enjoy listening to his stories," she insisted, and ventured further. "I think he really has enjoyed having me here, though, hasn't he?"

His mouth curved into a suggestion of a smile that was reflected in his eyes. "*Naturellement,*" he said, "and Grand'-mère too. By expressing an interest in *la cuisine, mademoiselle,* you have charmed her to your side also!"

"And you don't like that!" She spoke impulsively, guessing that would be his reaction. Although she already regretted having been so outspoken, it was too late to go back now. "You still resent me staying on here, don't you?" she said.

"Resent you?" He echoed her words softly, and the look in his eyes shivered along her spine like ice. "Did Grandpère not suggest that if I did not welcome your presence here, I am not the man he believes me to be?"

Old François's meaning had been unmistakable, but she did not like being reminded of it, particularly at this moment, and the flush in her cheeks warmed anew. "Monsieur – " she began, but Paul's shaking head silenced her, and he went on as if she had not spoken.

"And have you not already decided that I am exactly the kind of man he thinks me?" he asked, soft-voiced.

A frank speculative gaze travelled slowly over her features for a moment, then a large hand reached out and slid beneath her long dark hair. It cradled her head, resting on the nape of her neck, and the long hard fingers stroked her soft skin in a sensual caress that shivered through her.

"Monsieur Paul – "

Her voice trembled uncertainly in the shadowy silence, and he was half smiling. Smiling in a way that brought a tremulous uncertainty to her whole body, and yet she could not look away. She was drawn irresistibly closer without even realising it was happening, and the grey eyes held hers steadily.

"The difference between us, *ma belle*," he said, "is that Grandpère trusts you – I do not!"

"Trusts me?" Jesamine wanted so much to move away from the influence of that hypnotic and sensual caress, but somehow she had not the power to do so. "I don't – I don't understand why you should distrust me," she told him in a small breathless voice. "What is it that you're so afraid I'll find out?"

The caressing fingers tightened suddenly and became iron hard, holding her firm in their grip while he looked down at her with narrowed eyes that held the coldness of grey steel. "I am afraid of nothing, *mademoiselle*," he said, "but I do not like ghosts!"

"Ghosts?"

She stared at him as if mesmerised, at the strong tanned face below that swathe of thick untidy fair hair, and the grey eyes fixed suddenly on her mouth with an intensity that made her tremble. He pulled her towards him slowly, until his mouth hovered close to her own, his breath warming her lips.

For a moment he did nothing but gaze down at her and it was impossible, with him being so close, to judge the expression on his face. Then, briefly, he pursed his lips and brushed hers with a promise of a kiss that stirred her senses into chaos. "Take care not to raise them, *ma belle*," he warned in a voice barely above a whisper. "I do not like ghosts!"

Jesamine had no time to question his meaning, or to recover from the blatant seduction of that half-kiss, before he turned swiftly and was striding back down the stairs with her eyes following him dazedly. Heaven knew what ghosts it was he feared she would raise, but she could safely guess that Louise d'Armor, his mother, was one of them.

That unexpected meeting with Paul on the stairs seemed to have put everything else out of her mind, and it was only when she was on her way up to her room after breakfast that Jesamine remembered her decision to tell Monsieur d'Armor that she would be leaving the following week-end.

Paul had said little during breakfast, but once or twice she had felt his eyes on her and again experienced that odd little shiver of sensation along her spine. Possibly he had been waiting for her to raise the matter of her leaving, perhaps he was even anxious to have the fact confirmed, for he had left her in no doubt that he would be happier when she was gone.

In some way his admitted mistrust of her was more hurtful than annoying, and she wished she was not so sentient to the moods of Paul d'Armor. No man had come so close to completely undermining her self-confidence as he did, and it left her feeling horribly vulnerable and unsure of herself. The sooner she went home to the familiar and comforting company of James, the better. With James she always knew where she was, with Paul d'Armor she never did.

It was a threat of rain in the air that decided her to browse through her host's not inconsiderable library rather than venture out. She did not speak or understand French, but there were many beautiful first editions among the collection, she knew, and it was as good a way as any to spend a wet morning.

The library was at the back of the house, a big shadowy room, completely lined with bookshelves, and smelling, as libraries almost always seemed to, of a curious mixture of dust, ink and musty paper. The shelves ranged along all four sides of the room with space left only for four long windows, two of which looked out over the gardens at the back of the château and the thick belt of trees that half hid the far end of the building.

It was quiet, of course, and she felt a curious sense of invasion as she looked around the silent book-lined walls. Perhaps there was something about her ancestor, Charles Louis Vernais, among the hundreds of books, there was certainly no harm in looking. Although she was officially on holiday she still had an avid interest in anything to do with him, and a library this size was bound to cover all manner of subjects.

She walked around the room slowly, stopping now and then to admire the beautiful leather bindings with gold leaf lettering and she had circuited three sides of the room when she suddenly came to a stop, frowning curiously as she reached out a hand.

The book she took from the shelf was bound in beautiful red calf and its leaves were gold-edged, but it was its title that caught her attention rather than its beauty. Embossed on its spine in fine gold lettering were the words "*Le Château d'Armor*", and in smaller letters further down, the name of the author. Who the author was did not concern her at the moment, but the fact that there was a book written about the château itself was an unexpected find, and she turned it over in her hands eagerly.

It was doubtful it had been read above once, for the pages adhered closely together and were difficult to part, but she handled them with as much care as her impatience allowed. The paper was of good quality and the book must have cost a great deal to produce, so probably it was a private and limited edition. Perhaps, as with so many other treasures in the château, the present owners did not even know of its existence.

It was in French, of course, and therefore illegible to her, but it was quite lavishly illustrated and the drawings were excellent. There were even some photographs, although they were indistinct and of the sepia tone used by early photographers. Satisfied that she had at last made a find, Jesamine sat down in one of the deep comfortable armchairs the room was provided with and began to look through it in earnest.

The illustrations gave her an even better idea of the construction of the château than actually staying there did, and her heart beat breathtakingly hard when she turned another page and came upon a drawing of what she recognised as part of the gallery upstairs – what would at home be called a landing. It showed the long panelled wall just beyond the head of the stairs, with the window at the far end, and there was no mistaking the location.

Her own bedroom lay only a couple of yards along on the other side and beyond, where it turned a corner, into shadowy darkness as shown on the drawing, was another wing of the building and other bedrooms, including Paul's. The illustration was clearly and explicitly drawn and an opening, not a doorway, in the dark wood panelling made sense of Charles Louis Vernais's escape right from under the noses of the revolutionaries.

Some mention had been made, when she was told the story of the escape, of a secret way out, but no details had been given and no one had offered to show her the location of the escape route. In her more doubting moments she had believed that the secret panel was merely a colourful embellishment to an already romantic story. But now that she had proof of it in her hands she could feel excitement coursing through her like an electrical charge.

For the first time she felt an impatient frustration at not being able to read French, for surely somewhere among those indecipherable words was the information she needed to work the ancient bolt-hole. Another turn of the page and the information fell into her hands – a smaller drawing of one of the ornate beading strips that dissected the panelling at intervals, and she pored over it eagerly for several minutes before she was convinced she could identify it.

There was no one about when she emerged from the library and she could not help feeling just a little guilty as she climbed the marble stairs to the gallery. Maybe she should tell someone before she went seeking the panel, but this was something she wanted to do alone and she quelled her uneasy conscience firmly.

The exact spot was less easy to identify than she expected, but she eventually located it. How the mechanism worked she did not really know, but she pressed her hands all along the strip of beading shown in the illustration and, after only a few seconds, stepped back with a soft gasp of surprise, staring at the gaping hole that suddenly appeared in the panelled wall. It was only a narrow opening and it released a smell of dampness and the must of age that was distinctly unpleasant, but its discovery was wonderfully exciting.

It was still difficult to believe, although priest holes and secret rooms existed in any number of old houses in England, and there was no reason to suppose the French were any less inventive. For several seconds she stood on the threshold of the opening, her heart hammering hard at her ribs, not quite sure what to do next.

A first tentative look inspired further boldness, and within moments she had summoned enough courage to step over the slight ledge and peer into the solid blackness. It looked to be a narrow passageway going off to her right and only a couple of feet beyond that what appeared to be a flight of steps leading downwards, she went no further yet but stayed with one foot still on the carpeted gallery and a hand on the edge of the panel.

It would be impossible to go any further in without a light of some kind, and she hesitated only briefly before going back to her bedroom in search of some means of illumination. The furnishings of the room yielded only a pair of tall blue candles in a silver holder and, after a moment's hesitation, she lit one of them, holding it for a moment until it burned more steadily. Its flickering flame looked very wan and feeble in the light of day, but no doubt in the deep gloom behind the panelled wall it would provide sufficient light for her to see her way.

There was still no one about when she left her room, but the panel was closed again, and she stood for a moment with an anxiously beating heart wondering who had closed it. There was no one about and surely if someone had closed it again, they would have waited to see who it was that had discovered its secret. Eventually she convinced herself that the process was probably automatic, and she once more pressed the appropriate place to reopen it.

It was as she stepped through that she realised how melodramatic the whole thing was. It was surely the most outlandish thing she had done in her journalistic career, and James, had he been there, would doubtlessly have counselled extreme caution. There might not be another way out at the other end, she had yet to find that out, and if there wasn't then her ultimate fate did not bear thinking about, but somehow she was firmly convinced there was, for Charles Louis had left this way, and so could she.

There was very little headroom, Charles Louis must have bent almost double to use it, and it was festooned with centuries of cobwebs. Also she had the horrible idea that there were rats lurking somewhere in the darkness, for she detected soft scratching sounds in the darkness ahead.

She started visibly and the candle flame flickered when the panel behind her closed with a barely audible thud, but she was not to be deterred now, not with the chance of actually following in Charles Louis's footsteps, and she felt a thrill of excitement as she started off. The descending steps loomed before her almost at once and she stared down into the total pitch blackness, shivering in her thin summer dress.

The descent seemed endless, but the steps gave way at last to a long vaulted passage and she stood for a moment and peered ahead before going on. Heaven knew where she was, but so far she felt she must still be in the confines of the château, the passage ahead possibly led to somewhere outside the building itself, somewhere in the grounds, perhaps.

Having come so far there seemed no point in turning back now, so she went on, her footsteps swishing coldly on the stone floor, and eventually came up against a dead end, a stone archway that looked as if it should have had a door set in it, only it hadn't.

There was nothing so subtle here as a carved beading, but a plain iron ring set against the stone archway, that yielded only when she set the candle down and used both hands to pull on it. The resulting creaks and cracks set her heart hammering fearfully, but at last the seemingly solid wall swung outwards and away from her, and she drew in a long deep breath, her eyes closed as she enjoyed the comparative freshness of the air.

There was daylight too and she had no further need of the candle, so she blew out its flickering flame and looked about her. The sweet heady smell of incense gave her her first clue, even before she stepped through the opening, and she was not too surprised to find herself in a small church, somewhere just behind the altar and partially concealed by the ornately carved rood-screen. There was no one about and she guessed it was much less often used than it once had been, for she felt certain that she was in the private family chapel of the d'Armor family.

She felt undeniably excited as she walked round through the chancel and into the nave, for she was without doubt treading the very same path that her intrepid ancestor had taken to avoid the revolutionaries at his door, and somehow it seemed the most important discovery she had yet made.

There was a chill, still silence about her that held the sadness of ages, but she refused to be overawed by it, and walked on, drawn by the only sign of life in the little church, beside herself – flickering candles and a huge copper vase filled with roses.

There were plaques all round the walls, bearing names and dates, memorials to past d'Armors, but only one had candles before it and that copper vase with its glorious display of summer roses. It was a shrine rather than simply a plaque as the rest were, and she simply had to know who it was for.

She crossed the nave and noted as she did so the rich velvet upholstery on the pews and the matching hassocks. It was a little gem of a church, but catered as much for the bodily comfort of its worshippers as for their spiritual well-being.

There was no other light in the church but the daylight that came in through the elaborate stained glass windows and the flickering glow of the candles below the plaque, so that she stood on tiptoe to read the inscription. It was only a small oval of lighter stone set in the sombre granite walls, and seemed to be comparatively recent, and in a less ornate script than most of the older tablets.

"LOUISE CLOTHILDE", she read in a small breathless whisper, "beloved only child of François d'Armor and his wife Clothilde. 1920 – 1942."

It was such a simple inscription and infinitely touching when one counted the few years between the two dates, and Jesamine looked at it for a long time, trying to imagine what had happened to this other Louise, who had been Paul's mother. Wondering too, why he went to such pains to keep her from finding out about her.

She gazed up at the tablet for quite a long time, drawn by some aura that seemed always to surround the name of Louise d'Armor, and wondering if she would ever know the truth about her. Sighing deeply, she turned, ready to make her way back via the château gardens rather than return through that chill tortuous route of Charles Louis's.

As she turned someone stepped out from the shadows beside the low arched door, and stood facing her, a bright angry glitter in his steel grey eyes. "So, *mademoiselle*," Paul d'Armor said in a softly menacing voice, "you still pry into matters that do not concern you!"

CHAPTER SIX

"PAUL!"

The name came from her lips in a stunned whisper, and Jesamine did not even notice the unaccustomed familiarity of it, only stared at him as if he was some ghost raised from those dozens of names around the walls. Her heart beat so hard that she felt breathless as she stood in the cool shadows of the little church and looked at him.

She had not expected to see anyone, least of all Paul d'Armor, and her mind raced wildly as she sought for words to explain her being there. Heaven knew how long he had been watching her from the shadows beside the door, but he must have seen her looking at the memorial plaque in the wall, and his anger was in no doubt.

He gave her no time to say anything else but his name, but raked his eyes over her slim figure. They noted the damp smears of mould from the passage walls on the light skirt of her dress, and the fine wisp of cobwebs that veiled her dark hair where she had broken their barrier. There was a smear of damp dust on one cheek too which told its own story, and she knew she had no need to find words to explain how she came to be there.

"So, you have discovered the *route d'évasion?*" he said, and frowned impatiently as he always did when she failed to understand his language. "The escape route!" he repeated, and Jesamine nodded.

Her gaze went instinctively to the half hidden entrance to the passage behind the rood-screen. It was closed, she noted, and felt oddly trapped suddenly. "I – I found it by accident," she told him, then almost immediately regretted the very meek and apologetic tone of her explanation. "I don't really see that you can call it prying, Monsieur Paul!"

The grey eyes still regarded her with a relentless steadiness that was quite unnerving, and she began to wish that she had told someone after all about her intention. At least then she could not have been accused of concealing her exploration of the hidden passage.

"If we had wished you to see our private chapel we would have informed you of its existence," Paul said. "Since we did not, Mademoiselle Arden, you may conclude that we had no wish to have you probe so deeply into our personal affairs!"

"Oh, will you please believe me," Jesamine said in a small tight voice, "I'm *not* prying and probing into anything! My only interest is in Charles Louis Vernais, no one else!"

The grey eyes swept over her once more, steely and arrogant, and plainly unbelieving. "Your interest in Charles Louis Vernais surely ended when you completed your *histoire*," he said in a flat hard voice. "*Mais non, mademoiselle,* the unpalatable truth is that you are a journalist — your business it to pry and probe!"

"*No!*" She spoke much more loudly and vehemently than she intended, and she had for the moment forgotten where she was. Realising it suddenly, she looked around at the silent chapel and bit her lip in vexation for her own forgetfulness. "I can't quarrel with you here," she told him, "it isn't right!"

Paul neither agreed nor disagreed, but curled his strong fingers about her bare arm and drew her with him through the low arched doorway into the uncertain sunshine outside. It smelled fresh and damp after the recent rain and was incredibly quiet and peaceful.

The area was completely surrounded by trees, which

probably accounted for the fact that she had never noticed the chapel before from a more conventional approach. Around the church itself the ground was cleared, and one look was enough to tell her that this was the private burial ground of the d'Armors' that Père Dominic had told her about.

White marble tombs gleamed wetly in the pale sun, not ornately festooned with carvings, as she would have expected, but rather severe and cold-looking, while further back some much older gravestones, more humble in size, stood crumbling amid the cropped turf and towering chestnuts.

It was still not the place to raise angry voices, she felt, but Paul apparently did not share her view, for, still keeping his hold on her, he turned her to face him, standing for a moment in silence while he studied her flushed face. "Perhaps you would care to continue our – quarrel out here!" he suggested, his eyes glittering the familiar challenge.

But Jesamine had no desire at all to quarrel with him, much less to have him look at her the way he was now, with a suggestion of curl in his lower lip, as if he found her beneath contempt. She shook her head slowly. "I'd rather not quarrel with you at all," she told him. "It isn't necessary, and I – "

"It is inevitable while you persist in annoying me!" Paul informed her shortly. "You have the gift of always doing the wrong thing, *petite fouinarde*; of always being in the wrong place!"

"That's only your opinion!" Jesamine told him, stung to rashness by an instinctive need to defend herself, then gasped aloud when his fingers closed about her chin suddenly and jerked her face up to him.

"It is my opinion that matters eventually, *ma fille*!" he warned through tight lips. "Do not forget that, or it will be the worse for you, for be sure I can have you – removed, from my home should I decide to!"

"Don't *do* that!" She was angry, but she was also tinglingly aware of the sensation he was having on her senses while he held her, and she knocked his hand away, her blue eyes bright and angry as she rubbed at the marks left by his fingers. "I'm here at the invitation of Monsieur d'Armor," she reminded him, her voice small and unsteady, despite her efforts to steady it, "you seem to forget that!"

"I am unlikely to forget, *mademoiselle!*" he retorted, and Jesamine stuck out her chin.

"Oh no, of course!" she said. "You wouldn't have me here at any price, would you?"

Her hands were flexed tightly at her sides, and she was prepared for heaven knew what from him, certainly not for the short, harsh sound of his laughter. It glittered in his eyes, not as amusement, but bright and challenging as he looked down at her. "You mistake me, *ma belle!*" he told her flatly. "But you would have no time for probing and prying into things which do not concern you, if you were here at *my* invitation!"

His meaning was obvious and she had no time to respond, even had she the words to do so, for he reached out and pulled her into his arms, impelling her against the unyielding hardness of his body with a force that knocked the breath out of her. With one large hand he held the back of her head, his fingers twined into her long hair, while the other bound her to him inescapably.

Before she could even draw a breath, his mouth pressed hard on to hers, forcing her head back against his fingers, so fiercely demanding that it stunned her senses. Too dazed to do more than yield breathlessly in the first few seconds, she slowly realised how willingly she was letting herself respond to the assault on her emotions, and she began to struggle.

Her hands beat at his chest and she tried to turn her face away from him, but that iron-hard hand with its spread fingers held her firm and her struggles slowly died. When he did release her at last, she was too breathless to do more than stand and stare at him, breathing heavily. Her cheeks were flushed and her parted lips still burned with the fierceness of his kiss, so that she put a hand to touch her mouth with her fingertips.

A chaos of jumbled reactions stormed through her brain as she stood there looking up at him, and it seemed like an eternity before she could move. She was trembling like a leaf and her hands fluttered uncertainly as she let them fall at her sides – there were so many ways she could have reacted, and yet she could not yet bring herself to do anything.

She should have made some form of protest, perhaps even a physical one, but instead she stood doing nothing, while he looked at her with a disturbing darkness in his eyes that she had never seen there before. He drew a breath, as if he was about to say something, but Jesamine did not stop to hear what it was. Instead she turned hastily and went hurrying through the green shadows of the chestnut trees, not even knowing for sure if she was going in the right direction, only anxious to be away from Paul, and the disturbing effect he had on her.

It was more shock than surprise when François d'Armor made her the offer of working for him, and Jesamine stared at him for several seconds before she answered. "Work for you, Monsieur d'Armor?" she asked, and inevitably she looked across at Paul. "I – I don't quite see how I can – I mean, what could I do?"

The day before she had told him of her decision to leave, and she could not imagine why he would go to the lengths of offering her work with the idea of extending her stay even further. That unexpected and disturbing encounter with Paul in the chapel had decided her, and as soon as she got back to the house she had sought out her host and told him of her decision.

Old François had said little at the time, but she thought he was not pleased by her decision, although he had expressed an understanding of the reasons she had given him. Perhaps he had some inkling of her real reason, for he had more than once made some quite pointed observations on his grandson's attitude towards her. It was possible he could see how responsive she was to Paul's undeniable attractions and had his own reasons for encouraging their relationship.

Whatever they were Jesamine was wary of accepting anything that would bring her into continued contact with Paul. He was dangerous, as James had warned her, but she had only yesterday realised just how dangerous where she herself was concerned. Arrogant and ruthless, he would take anything he wanted, but it was doubtful if his own emotions could be touched very deeply.

The old man's bony fingers touched her hand lightly, reminding her that she had not yet given him an answer, and he smiled when she looked at him. "You have often expressed your alarm at the lack of security we have here," he reminded her, "and I am not so old that I cannot take good advice, *mon enfant*! I have decided that the whole collection of *objets d'art* – everything – shall be listed, as you advised. Then perhaps we will take better precautions for their safety, *n'est-ce pas*?"

"Oh, *monsieur*, I'm so glad," Jesamine told him, genuinely pleased that something was being done at last. "It's something that really needs doing!"

"I agree, *ma chère*, although I had not realised the urgency of the matter until you brought it to my notice."

He was smiling, and Jesamine wondered just what he had in mind. "So, Mademoiselle Arden, since you have concerned yourself with our treasures," he said, "why should you not have the privilege of making the *catalogue*?"

Jesamine stared at him for a moment unbelievingly. "You mean you want me to – you want *me* to do it?"

"Who better?" the old man asked. "You will accept, *n'est-ce pas*?"

Jesamine took a moment or two to consider. It was a once in a lifetime opportunity, and never again would a chance like that come her way. But it was also a tremendous responsibility, and she was not sure whether her capabilities were up to such a mammoth task.

Even if she did decide to gamble on her ability, there was still the question of staying on under the same roof as Paul d'Armor. It was impossible that she could ignore him, or her own reactions to him, and her heart was already hammering hard at her ribs when she contemplated such a situation going on indefinitely.

"It's very kind of you, Monsieur d'Armor," she told him, still waveringly uncertain. "You must know I'd love to do it, but – "

She looked swiftly across at Paul when his cool voice intervened suddenly. "But, Grandpère," he said, "Mademoiselle Arden is a journalist. Is it likely that a reporter would be interested in working with antiques? Also I am sure that *mademoiselle* is anxious to return to her home after so long. *N'est-ce pas, mademoiselle*?"

His obvious desire to see the last of her was something she found strangely hurtful, although she hastily quelled the feeling and responded instead to the challenge it offered. She looked at him down the length of her small straight nose, her blue eyes defying his opinion.

"On the contrary, Pau – Monsieur Paul," she informed

him, "I'm very interested in the idea!"

A tight smile recognised her slip of the tongue, and his eyes mocked her hasty cover-up. "Indeed – Mademoiselle Jesamine?" he said.

She ignored him determinedly, turning once more to his grandfather. "I'd be delighted to try," she told him. "I'm not an expert, but I think I know enough to list everything quite accurately. There's one thing I must be sure of first, though."

"*Mais oui?*" François looked at her enquiringly, and she in turn sought Madame d'Armor's attention.

"I'd love to work here, but I'll do so only if *you* approve, *madame*," she told her.

"*Moi?*"

The old lady looked so surprised that Jesamine felt a strange gentleness towards her suddenly. She was a proud and handsome woman, and initially she had given the impression that she was autocratic, but lately Jesamine had come to suspect that she was more often obedient to the whims of her strongwilled menfolk, for they seldom seemed to seek her opinion about anything.

"Of course you, *madame*," Jesamine told her with a smile. "You're the one most concerned with the running of the house, after all. Another person on the staff concerns you as much as anyone, doesn't it? Will it disturb you too much to have a stranger in your midst for a while longer?"

Clothilde d'Armor said nothing for several seconds, and Jesamine wondered if she realised how closely her grandson was watching her. There was a curious gleam in his eyes that was oddly disturbing and she wondered what he was thinking.

"I am certain you have the necessary – *connaissance* to do this work for my husband, Mademoiselle Arden," the old lady said at last. "I would be pleased to have you here.

Perhaps – " She hesitated briefly. "Perhaps when you are not engaged in your work we might discuss *la cuisine, n'est-ce pas?*"

Her approval would have been enough, but to have added that unexpected request for her company sometimes, Jesamine found rather touching, and she smiled at her warmly before she turned back to her husband. "So, Monsieur d'Armor," she told him, "I'd like to take the job – if you're sure you trust me with all those beautiful and valuable things."

She was thinking of Paul's remark that although his grandfather trusted her implicitly, he did not, and she wondered if the old man's trust was as naïve as his grandson insinuated. "Why should I not trust you, *ma chère?*" he asked, and Jesamine cast a swift glance at Paul.

"Perhaps you *shouldn't* trust a stranger so readily," she suggested. "Some would say you were taking a chance, *monsieur!*"

As if he followed her meaning, François too glanced at his grandson, shaking his head. "*Mon cher enfant,*" he said, "if you had been inclined to steal from us you could have done so by now. You could have taken things from our home and returned with them to your own, with no one the wiser, as you well know. *Non, ma chère,* I have long considered myself an excellent judge of character, also – " he shrugged extravagantly, "are you not one of our family?"

Jesamine did not commit herself on the matter of her kinship, not with Paul watching her, but she smiled at him, grateful for his trust. "I shall enjoy it enormously," she said, "though it's a big responsibility."

François winked an eye at her, and his smile was as mischievous as a child's. "*Mais oui,*" he agreed. "It will also prove to be a long task, *n'est-ce pas, ma chère?*"

It scarcely seemed possible that a week had passed since she started on her mammoth task of cataloguing the d'Armor collection, for she had yet to complete the contents of one room. Part of her time, of course, had been taken up with visits from François d'Armor, but mostly it was because Jesamine had not sufficient expertise to be confident. She could not tell at a glance the age and value of an article.

Being less expert she needed to concentrate more thoroughly and take more time over each individual item, and she often wished she had access to her parents' professional guidance. Not that she was unhappy with what she was doing, but she needs must be more painstaking.

She had received a letter from James that morning, in answer to hers telling him about her new job at the château, and it was typical of James that he had stated in no uncertain terms that he thought her quite mad. Why, he demanded, did she have to put her head into the lion's mouth?

That last had made her smile to herself, although she supposed there was a certain amount of truth in what he said. But whatever reasons James might produce for not taking the job, they were far outweighed by the satisfaction and pleasure she got from it. Nothing else she had done so far in her life had given her as much satisfaction as making an orderly inventory of the valuable paintings, furniture and *objets d'art* that had, until now, been shamefully neglected.

A glance at her wristwatch showed that there was still some time to go until lunch, and she put down the list she was making on the desk in front of her, running her fingers over the smooth beauty of its surface as she did so. Even the desk she was using for her work appeared on her list – an exquisite spindle-legged *escritoire*, beautifully inlaid with mother-of-pearl.

She stretched her arms above her head, then leaned back in her chair, enjoying a moment of relaxation with her eyes closed and her head tipped back, so that her long black hair hung like dark silk over the tapestried back of the chair.

The sun was warm and she would like to have been out of doors this morning. Not that she had any complaints, but she was accustomed to being rather more active than she had been of late, and there was much to be lost if she relaxed her concentration for a moment.

She heard nothing of the door opening, but opened her eyes hastily when a voice spoke from immediately behind her. "You are bored, *mademoiselle*?" Paul d'Armor asked.

The desk was near to, and facing, one of the windows, and the dazzling sun outside meant that she was momentarily blinded when she turned into the room suddenly. She could discern only his outline, not the expression on his face, but she thought back to the opinion he had expressed — that she was not interested in working with antiques.

"I'm not bored at all," she denied. "I was just relaxing for a moment, that's all."

"Ah!"

It said so much, that brief, expressive sound, and she had no idea what it conveyed in this instance. Now that her eyes were more accustomed to the softer light she could see his features more clearly, and she looked at him curiously, trying to find a reason for his being there.

"Did you want to use this room?" she asked.

It was unlikely, she knew, for this small quiet *salon* at the back of the house was seldom used. It was one of the reasons she had chosen it for her first inventory, thinking she would be undisturbed, although the past week had proved how wrong she could be.

Paul shook his head, seating himself carelessly on one corner of a lovely old Louis XV table, a liberty she viewed with some anxiety as well as disapproval. "I was looking for you, *mademoiselle*," he informed her, and she blinked in surprise as she looked across at him.

It irritated her sometimes that he still very formally addressed her as *mademoiselle*, and seldom with her name attached. She imagined the formality of it was intended to keep her firmly in her place and on no account would she suggest he used anything more familiar.

He had come from the vineyards, she guessed, judging by the state of his clothes, and again she wondered why he was there, since it was too early for lunch. His grey slacks looked dusty and there was a dark patch of mud on the front of his shirt where it clung damply to his broad chest. His thick fair hair, too, was less than shinily clean as it usually was, and she was reminded of how hot it must be in the fields.

There was the aura of hard labour about him, and he looked strong and earthy, and infinitely disturbing, so that she took a firm hold on her responsive senses. "Is something wrong?" she asked, and he smiled dryly, drawing one leg up to rest on the opposite knee while he quizzed her.

"Must there be something wrong because I seek you out, *mademoiselle*?" he asked.

Jesamine was uneasy, and she knew he recognised it, was probably aware of the reason for it. His tanned face glowed warmly from the heat outside, but his eyes were ice cool and glittered at her from below fair brows. Somewhere within her something urged her to smile and acknowledge the logic of what he said, but instinctively she lifted her chin, without really knowing she was doing it. Thinking she would feel less vulnerable if she was on her feet, she got up from the desk and stood beside it, looking across at him with evasive and uncertain eyes.

"It's rather unusual for you to come looking for me, that's all," she told him. "What did you want with me —

Monsieur Paul?"

It was sometimes difficult for her to remember to put the formality of a title before his name, for she was unused to much formality in her more familiar working world. She saw the flick of his brow when he noticed that barely perceptible pause, and the grey eyes mocked her silently for a moment before he spoke, pinpointing the near-slip unerringly.

"One day, *mon enfant*," he told her in his deep, quiet voice, "you will forget yourself and call me Paul!"

"And have you pull me up for it?" Jesamine retorted swiftly. "Oh no, *monsieur*!"

"Pull you up?" He repeated the words as if he did not understand their meaning, but she guessed he knew well enough what was meant by them.

"Your English is good enough to know what that means!" she said, and he laughed.

"Ah, *mais oui*," he agreed. "What I question is your certainty that I would – pull you up for using my name! I suspect the formality is meant to remind me that I should – how is it you say it? – keep off the grass, *n'est-ce pas*?" He gave her no time to recover from the explicit bluntness of the suggestion, but laughed softly and shook his head. "The letter you have received this morning from Monsieur Terril will have stressed the need for continued alertness, am I not right?"

It would be too embarrassing to admit it to his face, and yet there seemed little point in denying it. "James knows by now that I'm perfectly able to take care of myself, Monsieur Paul," she said in a determinedly steady voice. "In any situation."

"You sound very confident," he remarked, and swept a slow, searching gaze over her face as he spoke. "You are accustomed to – situations, *mademoiselle*?"

"I don't need a nursemaid!" She found his faintly smiling eyes too hard to bear and she turned her back to him suddenly and looked out of the window. Her heart was thudding hard in her breast and she stared out at the sunlit gardens, but saw nothing. "You still haven't told me why you came looking for me – Monsieur Paul," she reminded him over her shoulder.

She heard him move; the soft thud of a booted foot on the carpet, and a second later he was standing immediately behind her, the warmth of his nearness sending her pulses into wild, head-spinning chaos. "Again you hesitate," he remarked, so close to her ear that she felt the flutter of his breath against her neck. "Is it so difficult to remember not to call me Paul, *petite*?"

Jesamine's hands curled tightly at her side, and she did not dare turn her head in case he was even closer than she thought. "No more difficult than for you to remember to call me *mademoiselle*!" she retorted breathlessly, and only then remembered how firm she had decided to be about mentioning that.

"And you dislike the formality of that?"

It was impossible to carry on such a conversation while she still had her back to him, though she turned only slowly and with obvious reluctance. As she expected, he was much too close for comfort, and there was an expression in his eyes that she found infinitely disquieting.

Everything James had said came rushing back to warn her, but still there was nothing she could do about the rapid, urgent beating of her heart, or the sudden weakness she felt in her legs as she faced him. It seemed she had known that strong rugged face since the beginning of time, she thought wildly, and fought hard against the effect of steely grey eyes that seemed to see right through her.

"I have no objection to being formal, if that's the way

you prefer it," she told him, in a small and suddenly husky voice. "In fact it might be a good idea in the circumstances!"

"In the circumstances?" He was close enough to bend his head over her, so close she could smell the dust on his hair and his clothes, and he was looking down at her mouth with the same heart-stopping intensity he had once before, when she had stood barefoot on the gallery and he had so nearly kissed her. "The circumstances you are quite able to cope with, *mademoiselle*?" he suggested, and she realised with a flush of certainty that he was laughing at her.

She stepped back away from him, but could only go as far as the chair behind her allowed, then she was brought up short, her breath catching in her throat. "You know perfectly well what I mean," she whispered breathlessly.

Paul was smiling, his strong teeth almost wolfish in his rugged face, and she felt her heart fluttering nervously when he took a step forward, following her. She put her hands behind her on the back of the chair, glad of its flimsy support, but he reached around her and put his own big hands over hers, pinning her fingers helplessly with a force that startled her.

It brought him closer too, and the light pressure of his body aroused a startling sense of excitement in her that she hastily stifled. She could not claim that the situation was unforeseen, but she had not for one moment realised how she would react, and her own lack of initiative stunned her.

"Your friend warned you, did he not, of the kind of man I am?" he asked in a voice that shivered along her spine. "But you would stay on, would you not, *ma belle*? You tried so hard to make him return without you, and I think now perhaps you are sorry that you did so!"

Jesamine kept her eyes downcast, even though it meant she was looking directly at the vulnerable warmth of his throat where it emerged from the open neck of his shirt. "I'm not sorry at all," she denied, her voice whisperingly unsteady. "I – I had the chance of a holiday and I took it."

"And this time, *ma belle*?" he questioned her softly, his voice itself a weapon of seduction, and she felt her whole body trembling. "Why are you still here? To catalogue our collection of antiques?" He laughed. "*Mais non*, though you may convince Grand'mère, that is why!"

Jesamine struggled to free her hands, but his iron-hard fingers still restrained her, and she breathed erratically as she looked up at him. "I – I took a job with your grandfather," she told him in a small tight voice. "You know that's all there is to it – you know I'm here doing a job." Despite the chaos of her emotions, her blue eyes held a glint of defiance. "If you have any other reason in mind, Monsieur Paul, you – you flatter yourself!"

"*Petite minette*!"

The steely grey eyes still laughed at her, and there was no relaxing of those strong fingers that imprisoned hers, but she thought the shaft had gone home, and guessed it was not often that Paul d'Armor was spoken to quite like that – especially by a woman.

Then he bent his head suddenly and his mouth lightly touched the soft skin below her left ear. Her body tensed, there was nothing she could do about the instinctive reaction, and she was enveloped in a heady mixture of masculine scents that included some spicy after-shave as well as the dusty, earthy smell of the vineyards.

She leaned back, trying to evade that evocative caress on her neck, but it only brought him that much closer, and turning her head away did not deter him. "Will you please – "

Her words were cut off sharply when his mouth found hers and tipped back her head with the force of his kiss. Her lashes drooped instinctively cutting off the sight of those steely grey eyes, and she tried only briefly to turn her head again before his arms came around her, crushing her close against the fierce vigour of his body.

When he raised his head at last, it was to look down at her with an intensity that shivered through her like fire and ice. His mouth curved slowly into a smile, and it was when she saw that smile that she began to realise he had known exactly how she would react when he kissed her.

She put her hands to his chest and pushed hard, trying to rid herself of the touch of him, for while he was that close she could not guarantee her own strength of will. "I – I suppose you did that to prove something," she whispered huskily, and he laughed.

"What have I proved, *ma belle*?" he asked, his eyes bright and mocking. "That you are not as capable of taking care of yourself as you thought? That your James was right to warn you about men like me? You should have gone home with your lover, *jeune fille*!"

"James *isn't* my lover!" The protest sounded childish, even to her own ears, and she could see the glint of amusement it caused Paul. "Will you please let me go!" she breathed anxiously.

She tugged uselessly at the arms that still held her, but broke free only because he let her. She was angry, it showed in the brightness of her blue eyes, but there were other, more disturbing emotions stirring in her that she dared not allow to surface, and she could not move away even now that she was free of his arms, because he was standing too close to her.

"Will you please let me past?" she said, trying hard to steady her voice. "I – I want to do some more work before lunch time."

"*Mais oui!*" He stepped back a couple of paces and

allowed her to pass him, though she was obliged to brush against him as she did so. He watched her cross the room on legs that trembled like leaves, and perched himself on the corner of the *escritoire*, apparently heedless of its delicacy or value. "And after lunch, *petite*?" he asked.

Jesamine turned and looked at him, taken by surprise. She had forgotten that initially he had come seeking her for some reason as yet unspecified, and she could not imagine the reason for his present interest. "Why – I'll come back here and work, of course," she told him, frowning curiously. "Why do you ask?"

Paul shook his head, thrusting his hands into the front pockets of his slacks and smiling. "Because my grandfather has the idea that you would enjoy to see the vineyards and the cellars," he told her. "I shall understand if you do not wish to spend the afternoon in my company, of course, but perhaps you will be good enough to explain to my grandfather – he will find it more difficult to understand your dislike of the idea!"

To Jesamine the invitation was so completely unexpected that she stared at him for several moments with wide, unbelieving eyes. If she had had some intimation of what he had in mind when he came in, she could have had an answer ready, found something sensible to say instead of simply staring at him as she was.

Her natural inclination found the idea of spending the afternoon with him almost irresistible. It was the cool voice of reason, and James's cautious warnings, that told her how rash she would be to accept after what had just happened. She looked at him surreptitiously and wondered just what his own feelings were in the matter – whether he would want her to accept or if he was merely bowing to his grandfather's wishes.

It was the prompting of some unbidden sense of mischief.

that decided her to accept simply to see how he would react. "It was very kind of Monsieur d'Armor to think of it," she said, watching his face through her lashes. "I'd love to go – that is if you don't mind taking me, of course," she added, and saw him frown.

He eased himself from the corner of the desk and stood looking down at her for a moment, confirming her suspicion that he had neither foreseen nor wished for the answer she gave him. "You wish to go?" he asked, his brows drawn, and Jesamine nodded.

She could see now, she thought, why he had behaved as he did when he came in. Those seductive caresses and that kiss had been meant to deter her, to make her wary of being in his company, as he had said, but now that she knew their purpose she felt angry – angry enough to accept the invitation just because she knew he did not want her to.

"I'd love to," she told him, her eyes bright and defiant. "Unless, of course, Monsieur Paul, you'll find it an embarrassment being seen with me."

The cool grey eyes regarded her steadily for several seconds and she knew he sensed the reason behind her acceptance. He inclined his head in a brief, formal little bow, that to her expressed his dislike of the situation. "I am at your service, *mademoiselle*," he said.

He sounded so cool and perfunctory that for a moment she almost changed her mind. "You don't mind?" she asked.

He neither confirmed nor denied his willingness, but looked down at the dusty clothes he wore. "I apologise for the state of my clothes," he said in a flat, impersonal voice, "but it is hot and dirty in the vineyards and, like you, I have work to do." His eyes had the familiar challenging look when he looked at her again. "I will make myself available as your guide, *mademoiselle,* if you will accept me as I am. You will be ready at *deux heures, s'il vous plaît*. Two o'clock," he added impatiently when he saw her puzzled frown, and Jesamine nodded.

It seemed she was committed now, although he would obviously condone a change of mind. The outing could be interesting, even though she had to admit that a whole afternoon in his company could prove less than enjoyable if his present mood prevailed. If only, she thought, she was perverse enough to enjoy the knowledge that he was such an unwilling guide, it would have given her more satisfaction. As it was she felt more unhappy than defiant, and followed his tall, stern figure to the door with wide, uncertain eyes.

CHAPTER SEVEN

JESAMINE was in two minds whether or not to call off the visit to the vineyards with Paul, but his grandfather seemed so anxious that she should go that she had not the heart to disappoint him. He was certain she would find it very interesting, he assured her, and no one was better informed on the subject of wine-growing than his grandson.

Despite his insistence that she would have to accept him as he was, she noticed at lunchtime that Paul had changed into a clean shirt. His hair appeared to be slightly damp too, which suggested he had showered, and certainly he seemed less dusty and earthy than before.

Not quite sure what to wear herself, she put on a pair of slim-fitting blue jeans and a thin cotton shirt – it was too hot to wear very much – and tied her hair round, gypsy fashion, with a spotted scarf. There was evidently nothing wrong with her choice, for he nodded his head when he saw her, and she felt sure he would have made some comment if he considered her unsuitably dressed for the occasion.

From his manner through lunch, she suspected he nursed hopes of her changing her mind, but she refused to have second thoughts now and looked up at him with a gleam of stubbornness in her blue eyes as they got into his car.

They drove barely more than one kilometre along the Grosvallée road, then he stopped the car on a patch of sun-parched grass beside the road and got out. Fields of vines stretched away on both sides of them, and Jesamine wondered what one did when being shown over a vineyard, not to show too much ignorance of the subject.

She looked at him a little uncertainly, now that the

moment had come, but he paid her no heed at all at the moment. He did not even walk round and open the door for her, instead he took out and lit one of the king-sized cigarettes he smoked and, after a second or two, she too got out, standing on the grass border waiting while he gazed in silence across the endless vista of vines.

With the width of the car between them she watched him surreptitiously while he drew on the long cigarette, expelling the smoke forcibly from tight lips, his eyes narrowed. Looking across at her suddenly, he raised a brow, his eyes cool and steely grey. "I hope you have comfortable shoes," he told her. "From here on you walk, *ma fille*!"

He sounded just about as discouraging as it was possible, but far from having the effect he obviously hoped, it served only to make her the more determined. She smiled and answered him with a pert brightness that defied his attempt to deter her. "Oh, don't worry," she said, "I put on shoes that I could walk for miles in, if I had to." Walking round the car, she showed him the low-heeled casuals she was wearing. "These are all right, aren't they?" she asked.

Paul nodded without comment, drawing again on the cigarette before he reached out a hand to take her arm. It was an unexpected familiarity in the circumstances, and she felt her heart flutter warningly when his hard fingers curled into her soft flesh. But it was done only for the purpose of turning her in the right direction and then he released her at once.

"Come," he said shortly, "I have many people to see – I can only hope that you will not be bored!"

"Oh, but I'm sure I shan't be!" she assured him, then hastily avoided the brief narrow-eyed look he gave her before he started off across the field, leaving her to keep up as best she could. It was not going to be a very enjoyable afternoon, she reflected, if he continued in the current vein, and she glanced up at him as they made their way between the first two rows of vines. "You were hoping I'd say no, weren't you?" she asked, and went on before he could either confirm or deny it. "Or else that I'd change my mind!"

He glanced down at her, his grey eyes cool and calculating. "I should have known that you would not," he said. "Though you will find little enjoyment in this heat, and it is very dusty and uncomfortable – I know, I have been out here for most of the morning." Briefly his fingers dug hard into her arm again, and made her gasp. "But you have your own reasons, have you not, *petite minette*?"

Jesamine pulled her arm free, but almost stumbled and fell on the stony ground as she did so. Rubbing her hand over the marks left by his fingers, she looked up at him angrily. "That hurt!" she declared. "And don't call me little cat!"

"Pussy," he corrected her, without a vestige of smile. "You are too small and soft to be a cat, *ma belle*!"

"*Why* didn't you want to bring me?" she demanded, ignoring the provocation for the moment. "I won't hinder you! You can simply act as if I wasn't here! Go off and do whatever it is you have to do, I don't mind in the least finding my own way around!"

"My grandfather expects *me* to show you whatever you wish to see, as you well know," he told her, and there was some expression in the steely grey eyes that puzzled her as much as his words did. It was as if he expected her to read something more into his answer than was actually said, and she looked up at him curiously.

"I don't – *know* anything," she denied, watching his face. "Not even why you're so resentful about bringing me to see the vineyards!"

He made no reply but simply looked at her meaningly

from the corners of his eyes before acknowledging the casual salute of a short dark-haired young man who was working along one of the rows of vines. "*Bonjour*, Georges!"

They conversed for a few moments in rapid incomprehensible French, but the man's dark appreciative eyes followed her as she walked beside Paul, and his knowing smile as they left him had a disquieting effect on her confidence.

She had some difficulty in keeping up with Paul over the stony ground, for his stride was far longer than she was capable of and, almost inevitably, she went sprawling suddenly. It had been bound to happen sooner or later and she wondered hazily if he had realised it. Paul in this curiously malicious mood was a new experience for her, and she felt suddenly and alarmingly vulnerable.

For a second or two she lay breathless and face down on the dusty ground, feeling incredibly foolish because she knew the incident had been witnessed by the dark-eyed Georges and his fellow workers. But before she could recover her breath sufficiently to get to her feet two large hands spanned her slim waist and lifted her clear of the ground, like a puppy, and set her firmly on her feet again.

"Are you hurt?" His voice was unexpectedly solicitous, though she barely noticed it in her embarrassment.

He could have taken her hands and helped her to get up, or lifted her by her arms, but to haul her up bodily with his hands around her waist lent even further indignity to her position, and she found it hard to forgive him that. She sensed watching eyes and heard the murmur of voices on the hot dusty air, and her cheeks flushed hotly as she brushed the dust from her jeans, feeling oddly tearful for some reason she could not quite explain.

"No, I'm not hurt," she told him in a small tight voice, and brushed hard at her dusty jeans with both hands. She refused to look around her at the moment or at him. "Not in body, at least!"

"*Comment?*"

The steely grey eyes quizzed her steadily, until she was almost convinced he did not know what she meant, and she shook her head. "It doesn't matter," she told him huskily. "But please go on without me. I can't keep pace, and I'm getting very hot and out of breath."

"So soon?" He eyed her slim shape in jeans and the thin cotton shirt, and his mouth twitched briefly as if in amusement. "Grandpère, it seems, misjudged your stamina, *ma chère*! Do you wish me to drive you back to the château before I continue?"

Jesamine did answer immediately. She did not want to go back – to yield to his particular kind of blackmail, but he was right about her not having the stamina for it. Tramping over hot dusty fields at the pace he set was impossible for her, and it was certainly not enjoyable.

She looked up at him, far more reproachful than she knew, and searched his face for the truth. "You'd prefer that, wouldn't you?" she asked, and was troubled because it seemed to matter so much.

Paul did not commit himself but watched her steadily without really looking at her, she felt. "I do not attempt to influence you, *ma chère*," he told her coolly. "If you wish to continue we will get on."

Jesamine looked around her, angry and unhappy, not seeking anything except a solution to her immediate problem – whether or not it was worth getting hot and dusty u st to stay in the company of a man who made it pretty clear he would rather she was not there.

Almost unconsciously her gaze happened on the young man he had addressed as Georges, working further along the row, and briefly she saw one eyelid close, a half smile gleam in the dark eyes. She almost laughed at the nerve of him, right under his employer's nose, and without quite knowing why she did it, she looked up at Paul enquiringly.

"Perhaps," she said in a deceptively meek voice, "one of your field workers could show me around instead – then I shouldn't be taking up all your time, Monsieur Paul."

For a second only Paul stared at her uncomprehendingly. Then he too looked along the row of vines to where Georges still gave only half his attention to what he was doing, and his eyes narrowed, a tightness showing at the corners of his mouth when he looked down at her again.

"Oh, *mais non, ma fille*," he said in a hard quiet voice. "I do not pay my workers to play guide to every pretty girl who comes along! If you wish to continue, I will conduct you, my people have other things to do!"

"I merely thought – " Jesamine began, but he gave her no time to finish her explanation. His strong fingers curved around the top of her arm and he drew her along with him for several seconds before he let go. For the first few steps he went at his customary long stride, but when she murmured a protest, he slowed his pace to a speed she could more easily match, though the tension in his step did not lessen.

He said little to her, but walked the length of the long field, stopping every so often to speak to the men and women working on the vines, and after a while, tired of being virtually ignored, she protested. "You don't mean to enlighten me at all, do you?" she accused, and Paul looked at her with raised brows, as if her interest surprised him.

"You *wish* me to explain?" he asked, and Jesamine frowned.

"Yes, of course I do!" she said. "That's why I'm here, isn't it?"

"Ah – *oui*?"

She looked at him steadily and her heart fluttered uneasily in her breast. Once more his tone suggested far more than his words, and she was determined now to know what was behind those veiled implications. "It *is* why I'm here, Monsieur Paul," she insisted quietly. "Whatever other ideas you might have!"

"Ideas?" His tone dared her to name the ideas, but gave her little time to do so. He shrugged lightly. "If you wish to learn about wine, *ma fille*, you shall!" he told her.

"Thank you!"

He explained, at length, the cultivation of particular grapes to produce a particular wine; the importance of vine and soil combined to impart just the right flavour to the finished product, and she followed as best she could. He told her the process that turned grapes into sparkling wine, and how the labelling of wines in France was strictly controlled, in some cases remarkably detailed.

"For instance," he said, "some vintage wines have not only the château of origin, but the *clos* too."

"The – *clos*?" She hesitated to ask for a translation, but he merely looked resigned as he answered.

"The particular plot of ground on which the grapes were grown," he explained. "It is important when a wine is described not only to show the name of the château that grows the wine, but the *clos* too."

"Oh, I see."

She was impressed by the effort that went into ensuring that the connoisseur knew exactly what he was getting when he ordered a particular vintage. "Do you – does the Château d'Armor produce a vintage wine?" she asked, and Paul gave her such a long hard look that she thought he suspected sarcasm.

"*Mais naturellement!*" he told her. "Château d'Armor is one of the best wines produced in the Val du Loire! Connoisseurs all over the world know the 1967 vintage as one of the best ever produced!"

She had to be impressed, for he spoke with such fervour, and she had no reason to suppose he was not telling her the truth. Looking for a moment at the rugged face with its crown of thick fair hair, she felt a curious curling sensation in her stomach. It would be so easy to fall in love with him, and yet so unwise.

"It's fascinating," she said, bringing herself hastily back to earth. "I never realised quite how much effort goes into producing a bottle of wine. Is there more I can see?"

He hesitated for a moment, then shrugged, as if he saw no alternative, and once more she experienced that inexplicable sense of hurt. "Do you also wish to see the *caves*?" he asked, and translated at once when he saw her look puzzled. "The cellars, *petite idiote*!"

Much as she was tempted, she refused to be drawn into quarrelling with him. "I'd very much like to see the cellars, please," she told him in a voice that could have left him in no doubt how she felt about being called a little fool, and once more he merely shrugged, as if he had no option.

"*Très bien*," he said. Following him back along the rows of vines, she almost stumbled and he turned his head and looked down at her with an expression she did not quite understand. "You do not mind if I do not take your arm?" he asked, apparently quite serious, and Jesamine blinked at him uncertainly.

Once again she felt he was referring to something he expected her to understand, but which puzzled her absolutely, and she shook her head as she tried to imagine what he was alluding to. "No, I don't mind," she told him, her voice betraying her uncertainty.

She was all too well aware of the interested and speculative eyes that followed them as they made their way back to the road, and her quick look around showed plainly how she felt. She was wary of him, more wary than she had ever been, without knowing why and she caught up with him as they reached the end of the row.

"Ah, but of course you would prefer that I attend you like a lover, hmm?" he suggested. "It is why you are here, *n'est-ce pas*? To – create an impression!"

Jesamine was too stunned to say anything for several seconds, she simply stared at him. They had come to a halt opposite where an opening gave access to the road and she turned to face him, shaking her head slowly and trying to understand him. "I haven't the remotest idea what – impression you think I'm trying to create," she told him in a voice that was low and husky with uncertainty, "but you seem to have something on your mind about why I came out here with you."

She wished they could have had this incredible conversation somewhere a little less public, and it crossed her mind to wonder whether he had ever brought women visitors here before and whether she was automatically being classed in the same category. Then she dismissed it as unlikely, for the kind of women she imagined would attract Paul d'Armor were not the kind to stumble around in the dusty fields with him.

"You came to see the vineyards?" he asked, and laughed shortly. "Do you think I do not know why you came, *ma belle*? Or why Grandpère arranged this *visite*? Do you think I am such a fool that I do not know what he had in mind for me? And you, who so willingly – co-operate?"

Jesamine's legs felt oddly weak suddenly, and there was a curling sensation in her stomach that disturbed her strangely. She had given little thought to old François's suggestion that she came to see the vineyards in the company of his grandson, other than the obvious one – not until now, and now she could not even think about what Paul's idea might be without wanting to curl with embarrassment.

"Monsieur d'Armor knew I'd be interested in seeing all this," she told him, encompassing the endless panorama of vines with the sweep of one hand. "That's all!"

"And you are prepared to walk around in the hot sun, becoming dusty and *débraillée*, only to look at this?" he asked, making it obvious he did not believe her. "Are you then writing an *histoire* on the growing of the grape, Mademoiselle Journaliste?"

Jesamine flushed. She had had enough and her blue eyes sparkled with anger, her hands tightly curled so as not to hit out at that strong scornful face that doubted every word she said. "I don't know what your grandfather had in mind when he arranged this," she told him in a small tight voice, "but whatever it was, as far as I'm concerned my only interest is in the vineyards, *monsieur, not* in my guide!" She looked at him as steadily as her shaking anger allowed her to, and he met her gaze, narrow-eyed and arrogant.

"You must know that my grandfather would like nothing better than to see me safely married," he said. "Do not tell me that it has never occurred to you that his reason for employing you was to put temptation in my way, Mademoiselle Arden!"

"Oh no!" She stared at him unbelievingly, her lips parted and a dazed look in her eyes that should surely have convinced him. More than once she had suspected that François d'Armor was encouraging his grandson to flirt with her, but she had never in her wildest dreams thought of him expecting anything more serious – she still could not believe it. "You can't seriously believe that Monsieur d'Armor would – you *can't* be serious!" she said breathlessly, and Paul laughed shortly.

"Are you so naïve, *ma belle*," he said, "that you have not realised you are being thrown into my company?"

She could not deny that with any conviction, and she did not try, but she would admit to nothing any more serious than a mild flirtation being in the old man's mind. "I had – I thought he might have – " She shook her head urgently. "I don't believe he meant it to be any more than a – a flirtation," she said, her voice shaky. "And certainly I hadn't even that in mind!"

Paul was looking at her steadily and there was a tight, humourless smile tugging at the corners of his mouth. "You misjudge my grandfather's knowledge of me, *enfant*," he told her. "He knows well enough that I do not simply – flirt, and he knows you well enough by now, I think, to know that anything else would be out of the question with you – is that not right?"

The grey eyes were cool and calculating and they moved slowly over her flushed face searchingly. "Monsieur Paul, I – "

She was silenced by the touch of his hand sliding beneath her chin, lifting her face to him. "You would not contemplate an *affaire de coeur*, would you, *ma belle*?" he asked in a low voice that shivered along her spine like ice, and Jesamine turned her head swiftly to avoid him.

"No, I wouldn't!" she said huskily. "And neither do I believe would you with me, *monsieur*!"

He did not deny it, but pressed home his point about his grandfather's intentions. "Then taking all things into account, *enfant*," he said, "Grandpère had only marriage in mind. For a whole month he has not considered you might be interested in the vineyards, nor have you expressed an interest in them. *Non, ma belle*, you do not convince me! My grandfather knew what he was about and you were willing enough to do as he wished and come with me! I cannot believe you did not know what was in his mind!"

"You can believe what you like!" Jesamine declared, angrily breathless. "I've no intention of inflicting myself on you any longer if that's the opinion you have of me! I won't embarrass you any longer in front of your employees!"

The depth of her anger seemed to surprise him and for a brief moment she thought he regretted his outspokenness. It even looked as if he might apologise, but then instead he indicated the parked car on the road behind her. "Shall I then drive you back to the château, *mademoiselle*," he asked, and she shook her head, angry but strangely tearful too, and resenting that above all.

"No, *thank* you!" she said. "Don't make a pretence of being polite, Monsieur Paul, it isn't in character!"

"Pre-tence?" His eyes were steely and his accent much more pronounced, and she realised suddenly how much she hated quarrelling with him. "You would have me *more* impolite by letting you go back alone?"

She was anxious only to get away now, and she shook her head urgently, her voice unsteady. "I'd rather go alone," she said. "I can find my own way!"

She thought for a moment that he might insist on driving her, she almost hoped he would, but instead he simply inclined his head in one of those slight, formal little bows. "*Très bien, mademoiselle*," he said in a flat hard voice, then turned on his heel and strode off back along the row of vines with his arrogant head high and the stiffness of anger in his tall figure.

Jesamine watched him go for several seconds, her eyes wide and anxious. There was a fluttering uneasiness in her heart that regretted the angry parting far more than she cared to admit, and she almost called after him. The remnants of her pride prevailed, however, and she shrugged, turning from the curious eyes that still watched her, prepared to face the long, hot walk back to the château.

Jesamine never really knew what decided her on a change of direction after she left the vineyard, but instead of taking the road back to the château, she turned right towards the village. It was no more than a few metres to Grosvallée and at the moment it offered a more comforting prospect than having to explain to François d'Armor why she had left his grandson after an angry exchange, and walked back rather than let him drive her.

The village's one narrow street was almost deserted. The smell of fresh baked bread from the little *boulangerie* tickled her nose pleasantly, and the old men sat, as they always did, outside the small café, taking their ease in the sun and comforted by endless pipes of pungent tobacco and glasses of *vin ordinaire*.

In fact it was the presence of the old men that deterred her from quenching her own thirst, for there was something in those curious old eyes watching her without seeming to, that made her unusually nervous. Instead she walked along on the other side of the street, strolling rather aimlessly, as if she was not quite sure what to do.

"*Bonjour, mademoiselle!*" She turned swiftly, startled for the moment, then instinctively smiled at the teenage boy who stood looking at her enquiringly. "*Puis-je vous aider?*" he asked, and she shook her head.

"Hello," she said. "I'm sorry, but I don't speak any French."

"Ah!" Dark eyes gleamed at her eagerly. "Mademoiselle is English?"

Jesamine nodded. She was a little dubious about responding to such an approach, but saw no real harm in it since the boy was young enough to be easily deterred if he became persistent. She was aware, however, that they were under observation from a middle-aged woman on the opposite side of the street, and a few seconds later the woman called across in sharp rapid French.

The boy did not go over and join her but instead called over, using his hands and a pair of very expressive eyes to convey his meaning. When he finished the woman shrugged, rather doubtfully, Jesamine guessed. She added what sounded very much like a word of warning, then walked off carrying a big old-fashioned wickerwork basket over one arm.

"Mama thinks me still a little boy," the youth explained with a wry smile, and rolled his expressive eyes. "I have explained to her, *mademoiselle*, that I am not only almost a man but also a very good guide. If Mademoiselle wishes, I can show her around Grosvallée." The reason for his interest was apparent now, she thought. He hoped to become her guide and perhaps make himself some pocket money. "Perhaps you wish to visit the *église*?" he suggested hopefully, and added hastily. "The church, *mademoiselle*!"

Jesamine remembered Père Dominic's mistrust of her the last time she visited the church, and she shook her head. If Paul had since talked to the old priest he would very likely regard her with even more suspicion should she go again. "Oh no, thank you," she said.

The boy looked so disappointed that her soft heart reproached her. "You do not need a guide, *mademoiselle*?" he asked.

She took a minute to consider. "Do you belong here?" she asked, and he nodded.

"*Mais oui, mademoiselle*, my father is *instituteur* here! Schoolteacher," he added hastily when he saw her frown.

She glanced both ways along the little street and turned back to him with a smile. "Is there enough to see to warrant having a guide?" she asked, and he nodded.

"Ah, *mais oui*," he assured her earnestly. "There are the places where the Maquis fought, *mademoiselle*, if such things interest you. I know from my father where these places are and what happened there!"

It was inevitable that Jesamine should be reminded again of her conversation with Père Dominic. It was her suggestion that the d'Armors must have been involved in some underground activity that had aroused his suspicion, she recalled. She was tempted, she had to admit, despite the heat of the day, to accept the boy's offer to take her on a tour of the places where the Maquis had fought.

She had sworn to Paul that she would not probe and pry into his family's affairs, but she could not pretend complete disinterest, and somehow she suspected that Louise d'Armor's death during the war had had more significance than simply dying in childbirth. Perhaps, by accident, she would find out.

"Very well," she consented with a half-smile, and the boy beamed his delight.

"My name is René Marais, *mademoiselle*," he informed her. "I am very pleased to meet you!"

"Jesamine Arden," she told him, and he bobbed his head in a small polite bow, his dark eyes smiling.

"I am delighted, Mademoiselle Arden!"

In the company of her young guide, Jesamine found herself further into the country on the far side of the village from the château, and walking through some beautiful shady woods. They were sun-dappled and silent, save for the occasional cry of a bird among the thick undergrowth and she could have enjoyed the scenery even without the aid of a guide.

René Marais knew his recent history, and it became more

and more obvious as he talked, that either Monsieur Marais the schoolteacher had actually experienced the stories first-hand, or had studied his subject well and been equally diligent in passing it on to his son. The stories were complete and detailed, and lost nothing in the dramatic nature of their telling.

The time passed so quickly that when she at last looked at her wristwatch she was startled to realise that it was more than two hours since she had left Paul in the vineyard. It was time she cut short the tour, interesting as it was, or the boy's parents might become anxious about him. When she suggested as much to René Marais, however, he pulled a rueful face and looked disappointed.

"I wished to show you the place near the bridge where the Nazi was drowned," he told her with youthful relish for gruesome detail. "It is a tale of mystery, *mademoiselle,* for no one will say the name of the collaborator, though I believe that they know – even my father!"

Jesamine shivered. "Perhaps some other time, René," she told him. "We really should get back now."

"*Très bien!*" He shrugged resignedly. "But I should like to be your guide again, Mademoiselle Arden," he informed her gallantly, and she thought he was not entirely prompted by the generous contribution she had made to his pocket money.

"I'd like that," she told him.

They were walking along the village street again when an elderly man spotted them from further along the street and came hurrying towards them. "Papa!" René exclaimed, and pulled a face, as if he would rather not have seen him.

Jesamine watched the man anxiously, hoping there was not going to be any unpleasantness because the boy had been gone for so long. "You didn't do wrong, taking me on this tour, did you, René?" she asked. "I mean your father does know you act as a guide when you can?"

"*Mais oui*," René assured her with a smile. "There is very little opportunity in Grosvallée, *naturellement*, but Papa is pleased that I show the independence – he encourages me!" His bright dark eyes twinkled at her wickedly for a second. "I think it is that in your case, *mademoiselle*, he would have liked to act as your guide himself!"

Jesamine barely noticed the compliment, she was watching the man as he came closer and thinking how much older he was that she would have expected the father of a fifteen-year-old to be. It was obvious, she thought, that those stories René had regaled her with had been experienced first-hand by his father.

The nearer he came the more obvious it became that he was not happy seeing his son in her company, and he lengthened his stride so as to reach them the sooner. René made an attempt to introduce her when he at last joined them, but he allowed little time for ceremony and merely inclined his head in the briefest of nods, then drew the boy to his side.

"I am aware of your identity, *mademoiselle*," he informed her stiffly, but in such excellent English that it was obvious why his son had such a good command of the language. "Père Dominic has already met you, I think – you are a journalist!"

So that was it, Jesamine thought a little dazedly. Père Dominic had revealed that she was staying with the d'Armors as well, she had no doubt, and informed the schoolteacher that she had been curious about the d'Armors' part in the wartime activities of the village. There was a traditional bond between the priest and the schoolteacher, she seemed to remember, but she was puzzled in this instance as to why the old priest had seen fit to issue a warning.

"I'm a journalist," she agreed, and met the man's eyes with a determined steadiness. "At least in more usual circumstances I am, at the moment I'm working for Monsieur d'Armor at the château."

"So I understand, *mademoiselle*," the schoolteacher said in a flat dry voice. "Monsieur d'Armor, like his predecessors, is noted for his hospitality!"

Something in his voice, the implication that she was in some way abusing that hospitality, brought a swift flush to Jesamine's cheeks. "I can't deny it," she said in a voice that she held determinedly steady despite a tendency to shake. "He's – they've all been very good to me."

The man's dark eyes held hers, slightly narrowed as he looked at her for a moment. "*Précisément!*" he said. He took his son's arm and inclined his head in a brief formal bow. "You will please excuse us, *mademoiselle*," he said. "My wife expects us shortly."

Jesamine concealed her hurt at the situation with a rather tight little smile. "Of course, *monsieur*," she said. It was seldom that she came upon such antagonism towards her profession, and she found it rather hard to accept. It gave her a curiously alien feeling, as if she had no right there, and she found it oddly discomfiting.

René, she thought, was as puzzled by his father's attitude as she was herself, and he looked at her anxiously, resisting for the moment his father's pull on his arm. "I may be permitted to conduct you again, Mademoiselle Arden?" he asked, but she had no time to answer.

Monsieur Marais spoke up first, firmly but politely. "I think not, René," he told his son, then explained briefly to Jesamine. "My son is a little young for such duties, *mademoiselle*," he told her, and firmly quelled René's half-voiced protest. "We feel it would be better if he did not undertake to act as your guide again."

There was little she could say. The man had made up his mind and she could scarcely stand there and argue with him on the right to employ his son as guide. René was young and his father must have the last word, but the man's mistrust was as puzzling and hurtful as the old priest's had been, and she wished she knew the reason for it.

"I understand," she said in a small voice, then smiled at René apologetically. "Goodbye, René. I don't suppose I shall see you again, but – thank you!"

She walked past them with her chin a little higher than usual, and it occurred to her that Monsieur Marais was watching her with a certain regret. He was not a naturally unfriendly man, she guessed, and his attitude towards her stemmed purely and simply from the fact that she was, or had been, a journalist. A journalist staying in François d'Armor's home – for that, she thought, was the significant factor. What prompted such reticence, the reason behind it, she had no idea as yet, but she could not help feeling that eventually she would learn, perhaps without even trying to.

It seemed cooler once she was clear of the village, but it was still very warm and there was almost no wind at all. It was later than she had realised too, and she wondered whether she had been missed yet. Even if Paul had already returned to the château without her, it was unlikely that anyone would actually worry about where she had gone since she left him, although certainly old François would be curious.

There were still people working in the vineyards, although there was no sign of Paul's car now and she wondered what explanation he would give his grandfather if he had returned without her. It was doubtful if he would be as frank about his suspicions to the old man as he had been to her.

Recalling his mocking disbelief that she knew nothing of

any plan of his grandfather's, she felt the same sensation of embarrassment as when she faced him in the vineyard, and she was suddenly unwilling to face him again, knowing he still believed it. Instinctively she stopped in her tracks and dropped down on to the sun-warmed grass beside the road, resting her elbows on her knees.

It was obvious, now that she thought about it, that Paul was trying, hoping to embarrass her into leaving, and the fact that he set about it so ruthlessly was what hurt most, no matter how she tried to be uncaring. Twice he had kissed her in a way that made her tremble just to remember it, but each time he had left her in no doubt that he was aware of the effect he could have and was simply amused by her reaction. Now, she thought, she knew his reason.

If he really suspected that his grandfather had some scheme to marry her off to him, which she could hardly credit even now, then she supposed his resentment was understandable to some extent, but it did not hurt any the less. If only there was some way she could discover exactly what the old man had in mind, she could act accordingly. Until then –

She sighed deeply and poked with the toe of one shoe at the dusty surface of the road, raising her head when she thought she heard a car coming. It would scarcely do to be found by some passing motorist, sitting there in the gutter.

Getting to her feet, she brushed the dust from her jeans, then started once more to walk in the direction of the château. The car was coming fast, and recognition came in the same instant that the brakes were put on hard, sending up a cloud of dust from its shrieking tyres.

Paul looked at her for a second through the window of the car, but said nothing, and after one brief, searching glance he restarted the car, turned skilfully on the narrow road, then drew up once more beside her. Jesamine had expected him to drive on and she watched him warily, her legs strangely weak suddenly, and a rapid fluttering beat to her heart.

Why on earth he should have come out to look for her after all those harsh accusing words he had used, she had no idea. He got out of the car and stood looking down at her, a curiously bright and anxious look in the grey eyes, a hint of frown drawing his fair brows together.

"Where have you been, *petite idiote*?" he demanded at last, and with such vehemence that Jesamine blinked for a moment in surprise. His manner suggested that she had not only been missed, but that he had actually been anxious about her whereabouts, and she felt less indignant than curiously excited by his abrupt question.

"I walked into the village," she said as coolly as she knew how.

Paul's mouth tightened ominously. "But you did not think to tell me of your intention?" he accused harshly, and Jesamine flushed.

Lifting her chin, she looked him straight in the eyes. "When I left you," she reminded him in a slightly unsteady voice, "you weren't interested where I went as long as it was well away from you! And I don't have to account to you for every move I make, Monsieur Paul!"

"*Zut! Vous –*" He made a determined effort to pull himself up, then took her arm roughly and half persuaded, half pushed her into the passenger seat of the car, slamming the door after her. Striding round the car, he slid in beside her, still in silence and still looking angry.

Jesamine had it in mind to question him about why he had come to look for her, but on second thoughts she wondered if he might simply have come in response to his grandfather's request, and she was reluctant to have it confirmed at the moment. At the moment she preferred to foster the illusion that he had come of his own accord.

It was as they approached the entrance to the château that she saw a couple of policemen standing beside the tangled wreckage of two cars, and she shook her head. How it could have happened on such a quiet, little used road puzzled her. It had apparently been a pretty bad crash, although most of the chaos was removed now and only the two guardian policemen remained with the wrecks.

"Someone must have been pretty badly hurt in that," Jesamine observed as they drove by.

"Several people," Paul agreed shortly, and she realised he must have passed it on his way out.

"How awful!" She looked back through the rear window and shuddered. "No one was killed I hope."

He did not answer at once, but drove in through the gateway to the château. "A girl was killed," he told her abruptly, almost reluctantly. "An English girl – she was taken to the Hôpital de Sainte Marie in Nantes and died there."

Jesamine looked at him for a moment with a curious sense of anticipation curling in her stomach, though heaven knew why. "Did you see it happen?" she asked.

"*Non!*" His voice was harsh and he still spoke as if reluctant to say anything about it. "I came along only a short time ago, when it was all over, but the police told me."

"Oh, I see."

He said no more, but Jesamine's heart gave a violent leap as she looked at the strong, rugged profile turned so determinedly to her. She thought she knew now why he had been driving at that breakneck speed when she saw him, travelling in the general direction of Nantes.

He had been told that one of the victims of the crash was an English girl, and he had thought of her walking back to the château alone. He had probably not even stopped to reason why she had taken so long to walk that far, but had turned the car around and gone like fury back towards the Nantes road to check on the victim's identity.

"You thought it might be me?" she guessed, soft-voiced, but Paul did not turn his head, nor did he confirm or deny her guess.

Instead he drove in silence down the tree-lined carriageway. But Jesamine sat beside him feeling suddenly warm and slightly lightheaded when she thought of him driving like fury to find what had happened to her. Relief at seeing her safe and well would account for that vehement demand to know where she had been and why she had not told him she intended walking into the village instead of coming back to the château.

She leaned her head back and watched him from the thick shadow of her lashes as he drove round in front of the doors. She said nothing more, for she knew he would never admit to having been concerned for her, but there was a faint smile on her mouth as he cut the engine, and she found her own certainty that she was right incredibly satisfying.

CHAPTER EIGHT

JESAMINE had expected the list of antiques she was compiling to take some time, but she was amazed just how long the list was proving to be, and her alarm at their being unprotected increased the longer it became. The d'Armors must be incredibly wealthy by any standards, but even François was moved to exclaim that he had no idea they were housing such a veritable treasure trove.

In the three weeks she had been working on it, she had completed only two rooms and barely started on a third, and there were any number of rooms yet to receive her attention. It would be a very long job, as Monsieur d'Armor had anticipated when he offered it to her, but she wondered if he had realised just how long. At her present rate of progress she could expect to take as much as another six months to catalogue the entire contents of the château, and she thought it expedient to mention the fact during dinner one evening.

Paul looked up curiously when she mentioned an estimate of six months, but she could not tell whether or not he disliked the prospect. Lately he had been less openly resentful of her presence, although he was still a discomfiting feature in an otherwise pleasant situation. Sometimes he teased her, but he had never again attempted to kiss her or to practise his particularly disturbing brand of seduction on her.

François d'Armor seemed completely unconcerned how long the job took, and she was once again driven to speculating whether he actually did harbour the kind of devious aspirations his grandson had accused him of. He merely accepted her estimation, nodding his head and smiling.

"Did I not inform you that it would take much time, *ma chère*?" he asked, and Jesamine smiled ruefully.

"You did, Monsieur d'Armor," she agreed, "but did you anticipate it being quite so long?"

"I had no idea how long it might be," the old man admitted cheerfully. "Surely it is of little consequence, *ma chère*?"

"Are you weary of the task, *enfant*?" Madame d'Armor enquired kindly, and Jesamine hastened to deny it.

"Oh no, *madame*!" she assured her. "I don't think I ever would get tired of it, no matter how long it took!" She did not consciously look across at Paul when she spoke, but when he caught her eye he had a half-smile on his mouth that made her heart flutter anxiously. "It's just that – " She laughed and shook her head. "I don't know, it's just that I feel – I sometimes wonder if anyone suspects I'm making the job last longer than it should."

She had not mentioned who was the most likely person to suspect her of such a thing, but she did not really need to – Paul would know she referred to him. "And are you – making it last longer than it should, Jesamine?" he asked, his quiet voice demanding attention as usual.

His grandfather clucked at him reproachfully. "*Mais non, mon garçon*," he told him. "Why should Jesamine do anything so – unnecessary, huh?"

Paul shrugged. One elbow rested on the table and his long fingers curled about the stem of his wine glass while he regarded Jesamine with a steadiness that she always found unnerving. "*Je ne sais pas*, Grandpère," he said. "The idea was Jesamine's, not mine!"

Her glance held reproach as well as defiance, and she saw the glitter of laughter in his eyes as he watched her from across the table. Even after more than six weeks under the same roof with him, she still found him the most disturbing man she had ever met, nor was she any more immune to the irresistible fascination he had for her.

"Monsieur d'Armor understands me well enough," she told him, and went on to explain, "It's just that I'm so afraid of missing something, or of putting the wrong value on something very precious, that I'm taking so long. It's really quite hair-raising at times, wondering if I'm making a complete shambles of it all."

"Oh, *mais non!*" old François denied firmly. "That I will not believe! You do excellently, *ma chère*, and I would trust no one else to do it!"

"Thank you, Monsieur d'Armor, you're very kind to say so!" She could not resist another glance at Paul, and the slight wrinkling of her nose was purely instinctive. She only realised how provocative it might be thought when she saw the glittering look he regarded her with.

"You need reassurance?" he asked, and she thought for a moment before she nodded agreement.

"I suppose that's it really," she confessed. "I'm not an expert, not like my parents are, and I'm only hoping that I shan't be – found out, I suppose. I don't think I've made any mistakes yet, but I still keep holding my breath in case I do!"

"But you will not give up?" he suggested, and she wished she knew whether or not he was hoping to hear her say she would.

"Do you think I ought to?" she asked, throwing the onus on to him, but he did not commit himself to a reply, only curved his wide mouth into a ghost of a smile and shrugged his shoulders, as if it was not his concern.

"You do not consider leaving us?" Madame d'Armor asked, and Jesamine thought how differently she would have asked that same question just a few weeks ago.

"Not until you want me to, *madame*," she told her with a smile. "I enjoy being here too much to give it up voluntarily!"

Paul, it seemed, still had something to say on the subject and she began to wonder if he would still take the opportunity to persuade her to go if he could. "Do your family and friends not miss you?" he asked, and Jesamine needed no prompting to realise that he asked the question because she had received a letter from James that morning.

Rather than answer at once she disposed of a mouthful of cheese first, taking her time, while he sipped his wine and watched her at the same time. "No one's pining for me to go back, if that's what you mean, Paul," she told him, and a raised brow suggested he doubted her.

"No one?"

His interest in what James had to say to her she found rather surprising, and even a little amusing, so that she could not resist the temptation to play up to him. "Not that I know of," she assured him in a voice that was as guileless as her gaze, and beside her old François chuckled his appreciation of the situation.

"Why do you not ask if Monsieur Terril in his letter seeks to coax her away from us, *mon brave*?" he asked his grandson. "Not – how is it? – beat around the bush!" He looked at Jesamine, frankly curious and much less oblique in his approach. "Does he seek to take you away from us, *ma chère*?" he asked, and Jesamine took a moment to answer.

"As a matter of fact," she said, putting down her wine glass and looking at it rather than at the curious faces that watched her, "James said he might fly over for a couple of days some time. He's due for a few days' break soon, and he rather wants to look around Nantes – he didn't have much opportunity before."

"But he will also want to see you, *naturellement*?" François guessed, and she shrugged with almost Gallic resignation.

"Almost certainly," she agreed, and wondered why she was so unenthusiastic about seeing James again.

It was not that she liked him any the less, but somehow she felt he was bound to interfere with her life as it was now, and she did not want anything to do that at the moment. She was happy doing a job she loved, despite a few moments of panic, and she had a kind of tenuous armistice with Paul that she did not want to see end in the way it almost certainly would if James came back.

François d'Armor was regarding her with his shrewd dark eyes narrowed and speculative, and there was a faint smile on his lips, as if her apparent lack of interest in James pleased him. "You do not sound like the – happy lover," he said. "Will you not be delighted to see him again after so long apart, *ma chère?*"

Jesamine knew exactly what he meant, although he had stopped short of asking the question he really had in mind, and she smiled at him over the rim of her wine glass. "I told you in the beginning, Monsieur d'Armor," she reminded him, "there's no romance in James' and my relationship, none at all. We're simply good friends, that's all. I've missed him a little during the past weeks, but I can't honestly say I've been pining for him. Nor has he for me, I suspect. James is much too sensible for that!"

"*Sensible!*" François echoed in a very pronounced accent, and shrugged his thin shoulders despairingly. "*Mon dieu! But what has sense to do with romance, mon enfant?* What has it to do with *l'amour*, huh?"

Jesamine's eyes were bright with laughter. The old man was such a determined romantic and nothing, it seemed, would change him. He was firmly convinced that James was in love with her and would believe no different. He looked at her and shook his head.

"You laugh, *ma belle*," he accused her with a twinkle in his eye, "but tell me, what has sense to do with *l'amour*?"

"Nothing, I suppose, Monsieur d'Armor," she told him, her laughter bringing a flush of warmth to her face. "But I've told you many times, there *isn't* anything like *l'amour* with James and me."

"Ah! So you have, *ma belle*," he agreed, and glanced quite openly at his grandson as he added, "nor with anyone at all, huh?"

Jesamine refused to be drawn into anything as dangerous as commenting on Paul's attitude towards her or hers to him, and she merely smiled and shook her head. "No one at all," she agreed. "I like it that way!"

"*Mon dieu!*" the old man murmured piously. "To think that I should hear a lovely young girl say such a thing!" He put his bony hand over hers and nodded his head as he studied her for a moment. "Maybe another six months of *la belle* France will teach you better," he said. "I will not believe otherwise!"

It was barely credible that the year was well into August, Jesamine thought as she made her way across the parkland behind the château. For sure the days were already a little shorter, but they were no less warm and sunny and she was still glad of the cool shade offered by the cluster of trees that sheltered the little chapel of the d'Armors.

It was more than two months now since she had first come to the château, and she felt remarkably at home there. Almost as if she belonged, she thought, and wondered if it was her connection with Charles Louis Vernais that enabled her to fit with such satisfying ease into his environment.

It was much cooler under the trees and she welcomed the shade after a day spent working in one of the smaller rooms where day long sun made it almost unbearably hot. She had finished work a little earlier than usual and refreshed herself with a bath and a change of clothes, so that she found herself with plenty of time to take a walk before dinner.

She never grew tired of the lovely walks the extensive grounds had to offer, and she was forever finding new ones. The little chapel in the clearing still remained more or less an unknown quantity for her, for she had never been into it again since that first time, when she had come upon it from the secret passageway and been surprised by Paul. She felt she should not go in again without a specific invitation, although once or twice she had been tempted when she had been walking close by.

She would like to look more closely at the little shrine for Louise d'Armor for one thing, for the girl still intrigued her, the more so because she had never been mentioned apart from that one brief word from the old priest in the village. It was incredible that she remained such a mystery, and curious that both the priest and the village schoolteacher had so determinedly shied away from contact with her once they knew she was a journalist and staying with the d'Armor family. There was definitely something about Paul's mother that invoked what Jesamine saw as a kind of loyalty of silence, and on the whole it served only to make her more curious.

The little chapel looked tiny and so tranquil standing amid its surrounding trees that she stood for a moment looking at it and wondering if she dared steal another look inside while there was no one about. Paul, she knew, was in his room washing off the grime of the vineyards and changing out of his working clothes ready for dinner, and he was the only one likely to have caught her.

The ancient tombs crumbling amid the trees opposite to where she stood had a slightly discouraging look, but she shook herself free of any fanciful ideas and walked across the clearing. As she opened the low wooden door of the chapel, its ancient hinges creaked and the old wood shushed over the stone floor as it opened so that she glanced over one shoulder, feeling strangely guilty.

There were yellow roses still before Louise d'Armor's memorial plaque, and the yellow light of candles flickered over the lighter oval stone set in the ancient walls of the chapel, but she did not go straight to it this time. Instead she walked around the walls, looking at some of the other plaques, unconsciously seeking those of Charles Louis Vernais, or Raoul Amadis Vernais, whom Paul so much more closely resembled.

She had just located that of Raoul Amadis when she heard a sound from just outside the little chapel, and looked around in sudden panic. To be caught there again would be unthinkable, and yet there was little hope of concealing herself for very long if whoever it was actually came inside. Once more she felt horribly guilty about being there when she knew that Paul at least would scorn her inquisitiveness.

Her one object was to get out again without being seen if it was possible, and at that moment she caught sight of the rood screen from the corner of her eye, and remembered that the entrance to the passage was behind it. Hastily, because there were easily audible footsteps on the porch now, she hurried across and ducked behind the screen.

She twisted the ornamentation that opened the panel, in a frenzy of anxiety when she heard the outside door creak and shush over the stone floor when it opened. She stepped through the opening quickly, with no idea who might have come into the chapel, and the heavy stone swung to behind her. It was only then that she realised she had no form of lighting with her – when she was left in complete darkness.

It was frightening, appallingly so, but she determinedly

fought down the sense of panic that welled up in her, and began to grope her way along the walls of the underground passage. With not even a candle to guide her, she stumbled occasionally and added to her fears, and she was shivering with something more than the cold dampness from the stone walls as she began at last to climb the steps of that interminable staircase leading to the exit on the gallery upstairs.

Her legs were beginning to ache as she stumbled at last up the last step and stood for a moment trying in vain to pierce the glowering darkness around her. The panel, she thought, had been not too far from the top of the steps, but she found it very hard to judge distance in the darkness and she could not really remember just how far it had been.

Using her hands to find her way, she searched along the wall beside her, where she knew an iron ring should be. There had to be some means of opening the panel from the inside, either an iron ring like the one into the chapel, or a lever of some kind, but she could find nothing so far.

She had come much further, she felt sure, than she remembered as the distance from the panel to the top of the steps, and she began to panic when her groping fingers encountered nothing but the harsh cold stone. Until, a little further on, she stopped, standing for a moment, helpless and suddenly terrified.

There must be some way of getting out, of leaving behind this interminable darkness, if only she could find it, and once more she sternly suppressed the panic that threatened to take over as she moved on again. Relief came from a direction she least expected it, when she was brought up short by the solidity of a stone wall across her path.

Reaching up with both hands, she sought some means of moving it and at last found a rusty iron ring and clung to it tearfully for a second or two in sheer relief. No matter if it did not take her through into the gallery, at the moment she cared only that she was going to be free at last of the creepy coldness of the passage, and she vowed never to enter it again.

It required more effort to move than she had needed before and by the time the solid mass yielded at last she was sobbing with anxiety in case it did not work. Then suddenly she was blinded by the influx of daylight, and she put a hand to her eyes as she stepped through the opening.

She did not stop to wonder where she was in the first instance but leaned back against the wall covering her eyes as the panel slid automatically into place again. Then, grimed and breathing hard from her earlier panic, she put down her hands and looked around her, realising with a start that she was in someone's bedroom.

It was a big, bright room, warm with the evening sun, and with a huge fourposter bed right beside where she was standing, its drapes hiding most of the room from her. A massive fireplace occupied nearly half one wall, and there was a desk and an armchair – a slightly untidy, comfortable room, and some discarded clothes over a smaller chair gave her her first clue as to whose it was.

She stood for a moment or two, too wary to move, and prayed silently that the owner was not still in occupation. It was a definitely masculine room, with no sign of a woman's occupation, and the only lone male likely to be sleeping in a room of this size was Paul. And that presented a whole new set of problems, if he was still preparing for dinner.

Her heart was hammering wildly, in a different kind of panic now, as she heard a door open somewhere out of her line of vision, then the soft swish of footsteps over the deep pile of the carpet. The smell of steam and a masculine scent of some kind reached her with the opening of the door, and she could guess that a bathroom led off from the far side of the room.

There was nowhere she could go now. If she tried to reach the door he would be certain to see her, and she could not bear the thought of his catching her sneaking out of his room. Nor could she face the prospect of going back behind the panel, even had she known how to work it from this side, so she simply stayed where she was, and hoped for an opportunity she knew was unlikely to materialise.

She could imagine easily enough what Paul would say when he saw her and, in this instance, she had to admit she was scarcely in a position to blame him. To find her, of all people, in his bedroom and looking dirty and dishevelled was the last thing he would anticipate, and she held her breath as she waited for him to discover her.

He came striding into view suddenly, and it was debatable which of them betrayed the most surprise. Seeing her, Paul stopped dead in his tracks, his eyes blank, stunned by the unexpected. Jesamine, for her part, was not quite sure what she expected, but certainly not the tall rangy figure that appeared in front of her suddenly, clad in little more than a silk bathrobe that clung to his damp skin and barely covered his knees. A virile, forceful figure that, even in the present circumstances, stirred strange and disquieting responses in her.

His hair was dishevelled and still damp, as if he had come straight from a shower without time to restore it to order, and his feet were bare, planted firmly on the red carpet as he stared down at her, huddled near the head of his bed. The grey eyes lost their glazed look soon enough and the first glimmer of laughter showed in their depths.

Jesamine's reaction, as she looked up at him, was a mixture of reproach and challenge that showed plainly in her eyes. He shook his head, ran both hands through the thick dampness of his hair, then stood with them on his hips, looking at her once more, and his mouth twitched with a suppressed smile as he spoke.

"You honour me, *mademoiselle*," he told her with a mock bow. "This is an unexpected pleasure!" He scanned the state of her dress and her face and hands, all liberally smeared with dust and mould from the passage. "But surely, *ma belle*, you are not always so – careless with your *toilette* when you *rendezvous* in a man's bedroom, are you?"

As well as embarrassment, Jesamine felt horribly vulnerable suddenly, and she shook her head as she sought to explain. "I came from – "

"I know where you came from, *ma fille!*" Paul interrupted shortly, his glance flicking briefly to the panelled wall behind her. "You have been into places where you have no right, yet again – and when I was beginning to believe I had at last trained you to behave!"

Jesamine flushed. It was quite bad enough to be caught in a situation like this, but to have him speak to her as if she was simply an annoying and inquisitive child was adding insult to injury. His first suggestion had been less insulting, though more provocative. It was not, she recognised, the best time to tell him that she had come through from the chapel, for that would be even less acceptable, so she saw no alternative but to offer nothing but an apology.

"I'm – I'm sorry," she said, wishing her voice did not sound so unsteady or so meek. "But you must know that I'd no idea I'd come out in – I'd no idea where I'd come out."

"*Non?*"

She flushed, her hands clasping the tops of her arms tightly, for there was an expression in his eyes as he looked down at her that brought a new, wild urgency to her heart's beat, and she shook her head slowly, without quite realising she was doing it.

"You know I wouldn't – you must know I'd never have come through here if I'd known you were in here," she told him breathlessly, and Paul said nothing for a moment, but continued to watch her with that steady, disconcerting gaze.

Then he reached out suddenly and with one fingertip lightly brushed away a tear from her cheek with a touch that shivered along her spine. She had shed tears of panic in that cold dark passage and he knew it, she thought – his next words confirmed it. "You would have come through any door that opened to you at that moment, I think, *ma chère*," he told her, soft-voiced, "even had it led you to the worst villain in France. Am I not right?"

"Perhaps." She made the admission reluctantly, and Paul was looking at her curiously.

"Did you know that this was once Charles Louis Vernais's room?" he asked, and for a moment she forgot her own present position as she became once more involved in the doings of their mutual ancestor.

"It was?" She looked past him into the big bright room. "I had no idea – "

"Or you would have come in here before now, hmm?" he suggested, then waved away her half-formed protest before she could voice it. He was smiling, a disturbing kind of smile that sent a warning shiver through her whole body, and made her hastily avoid his eyes. "He was *très séduisant*, as we have already agreed," he reminded her.

"Very – seductive," Jesamine translated uncertainly, and he smiled more boldly, wolfishly in that strong brown face.

"*Mais oui, ma chère*, you are learning!" He applauded her efforts with a hint of mockery. "He was fond of the girls and Louise Sutton was not his only *paramour* by any means – he had others in this village too."

Jesamine realised he was making the point to impress her

155

with the fact that he had insisted he knew Charles Louis far better than she did. From the beginning he had cast doubts on her vision of Charles Louis as the loyal lover of Louise Sutton, and she had not believed him because she preferred not to. She could have expressed the same doubts now, but somehow this time she did believe him. Why should she not? she thought a little wildly. Was not Paul himself cast in the same mould — unless appearances were deceptive?

"The French taste for *l'amour*, no doubt?" she suggested rather bitterly, and Paul shrugged, his eyes sweeping over her flushed face.

"*Possible*," he agreed quietly. "Does that trouble you so deeply, *ma chère*?"

She shook her head, glancing up at him as she did so, glad to see that the wolfish smile was replaced by another, more gentle expression. "It doesn't trouble me at all," she denied, "but it does disappoint me that he wasn't — loyal."

He smiled slowly, his eyes on her mouth. "One man, one woman?" he suggested. "Is that your ideal, *ma chère*?"

"I suppose so," Jesamine admitted defensively. "It's every woman's ideal!"

He nodded, pulling his mouth into a grimace as he did so. "But not that of every man, *chèrie*, unfortunately!"

She was not at all sure what her next move should be. It would be difficult to make a dignified withdrawal in the circumstances, but she could not stay there any longer, not with her senses responding so urgently to that curiously gentle look in his eyes. "I have to go," she told him huskily.

He was standing immediately in front of her and she would have to get past him to reach the door. Somehow she could not yet find the will to simply brush past him, and while she hesitated he looked down at her steadily. The soft pink dress she wore was soiled and one side of its hem had a ragged tear in it that she had not even noticed until now, but even with a smear of dust across one cheek and her hair dishevelled there was an almost fragile look about her that was appealing.

"You think I will let you go now that you are here?" Paul asked in that deep, seductive voice she remembered from once before, and she looked up swiftly, her eyes wide and wary.

She tried to judge what he would do if she attempted to just walk past him, and decided he would in all probability merely laugh at her, and let her go. "I'm going to my room," she said in a small breathless voice. "Please move out of my way, Paul!"

He said nothing, but as she stepped to one side and tried to pass him his right hand reached out and grasped her arm, pulling her close against him. She was facing him, their arms touching and his face only inches from hers, that spicy, masculine scent mingling with the warmth of his body and having the most devastating effect on her senses.

"Not yet," he said, barely above a whisper.

"Paul –"

She could feel her legs shaking like leaves and threatening to collapse under her, and she looked up only to find the expression in his eyes even more disturbing than her own imagination. She was trembling and unresisting as, wordlessly, he drew her round in front of him and slid his arms around her, drawing her still nearer until she seemed almost moulded to the firm vigour of his body, pressed closer by the pressure of his strong hands at her back.

She lifted her mouth to him instinctively, half closing her eyes as the rugged dark features filled her vision for a moment before his searching mouth pressed deep into her own. Breathless, as if she had been running hard, she lifted her arms and put them around his neck, laying her forehead against his chest while he kissed the soft skin at the nape of her neck and beside her ear.

Slowly she rolled her head back, shaking back her long hair and closing her eyes again in sensuous pleasure as he pressed his lips to the smooth softness of her throat, discovering a kind of delirious excitement she had never known existed until now.

There was a warmth, a tingling awareness that her own body responded to instinctively as he held her, a growing need to love him that was shattering in its intensity. "*Chèrie!*" She stirred, looking up at him with a glowing warmth in her eyes that lent them a darkness they did not normally have, and she smiled. "*Tu es belle!*" he whispered. "You are lovely, *ma chère*!" He pulled her close again and kissed her with an abandon that took her breath away.

Opening her eyes, she looked at him, her heart beating so fast that she could only manage a small, breathless-sounding voice. "I know – " she began, and laughed shakily. "I know I'm being quite – idiotic," she told him, her hands placed side by side on the breadth of his chest, "but at the moment it doesn't seem to matter."

Paul laughed. A deep, satisfied sound that vibrated through her as she watched it reflected in his steel grey eyes. "Then be a complete *idiote, ma chère*," he said, "and come to dinner with me!"

"Dinner?" She looked at him a little dazedly, vaguely remembering that it must be close on dinner time already. "But aren't we supposed to be having dinner very soon?" she asked.

She was still held firmly in his arms and his very informal garb did not yet strike her as she looked up at him, unaware of anything at the moment but the thrill of being close to him, and Paul bent and touched her mouth lightly with his own, smiling and shaking his head. "I wish to drive you into Nantes and have dinner there, *ma belle*," he told her.

"Will you come with me?"

Jesamine looked up at him in silence for a moment, brought down to earth at last by the need to make a decision. At any other time before this she would have viewed his invitation with extreme suspicion, wondering what lay behind it. Now she was anxious to accept, but only if she was sure of his reasons for asking her, and her blue eyes searched his face, a slow, anxious search that took in every familiar aspect of it.

"I'd love to come if you really want me to," she said in a small unsteady voice that showed her uncertainty, and he pulled her close again, smiling down at her.

"*Mais naturellement* I want you to come!" he said. "Why else would I ask you, *ma chère*, hmm?" She did not answer and after a second or two he lifted her chin and kissed her mouth with a gentleness that was as devastating as his former passion had been. "Why do you doubt me, Jesamine?" he asked, and she shook her head.

"Perhaps because I don't — I can't quite understand you," she confessed at last in a small voice, and he laughed softly, shaking his head.

"Then do not try, *petite*!" he said.

The dizzying moment of uncaring was over, though she was reluctant to leave his arms. Only now she was too aware of the thinness of the silk robe and of the warm vigour of the body beneath it, of the intimacy of their situation, close together in the privacy of his bedroom, and she had an uneasy suspicion at the back of her mind that she was perhaps following rather too closely in the footsteps of Louise Sutton after all.

"Paul — "

"You will come?" He gave her no time to finish, and the familiar challenging look was in his eyes again as he looked down at her. It was a look she found hard to resist, no matter how foolish she might be and she nodded.

"I'll come," she said huskily. "But I must – "

Paul silenced her with a kiss. "You must remove the dust of ages, *ma chère*," he told her with a laugh. "The rest you may leave to me!"

CHAPTER NINE

It was while she was changing her dress that it suddenly occurred to Jesamine that by agreeing to go out to dinner with Paul she had taken a very definite step in what James would call the wrong direction. She had been so sure that she could control the situation between herself and Paul and until now she had managed to remain, if not completely unaffected, at least fairly firmly in control of her emotions.

Finding herself so suddenly and unexpectedly in his bedroom like that had put her at a disadvantage, and Paul's reaction had not been quite what she expected. The fact that he would take advantage of the situation the way he had was something she could have anticipated, but the invitation to have dinner with him seemed, on reflection, an uncharacteristically impulsive gesture for someone as cool and calculating as she had thought Paul to be. It was that sudden and totally unexpected invitation that was making her wary; she could not help wondering exactly what had prompted it.

Surveying her reflection in the mirror, she sighed. Maybe she was being an utter fool for accepting, James would surely say she was, but she had been unable to resist it, and there seemed little she either could or wanted to do about the growing intensity of her feelings for Paul. Having dinner with him was likely to undermine the last shreds of her resistance, but at the moment there was nothing she could do about that either.

From the alcove beside the window Louise Sutton looked at her with sober blue eyes, and it was almost like looking into a mirror. Louise had loved and lost, but there was no way of knowing whether she had been heartbroken or merely resigned when her lover returned to his own country and married a French wife. Not even her letters revealed so much about her. Perhaps she had realised that one man, one woman was not possible in her case and had accepted the fact.

Jesamine stood looking at the miniature for a second or two, as she often did, for she never failed to be fascinated by the pretty little English girl who had forged a link all those years ago between her own family and the autocratic d'Armors. She reached out suddenly and touched the small painted face gently with a fingertip.

"Oh, Louise," she whispered, "you certainly made things hard for me when you took a d'Armor for your lover – but for you I wouldn't be here."

The sound of a door closing along the gallery somewhere snatched her back to reality and she turned from the fascination of Louise Sutton to pick up her bag from the bed. A last look in the mirror confirmed her suspicion that there really was a sombre darkness in her blue eyes that was completely at variance with the way a girl ought to feel going on a date with someone like Paul d'Armor, and she shook back her long hair in a gesture of impatience. She was an intelligent young woman and should surely be capable of enjoying an evening in the company of a man without letting herself be fooled into falling hopelessly in love with him – even if he was Paul d'Armor.

She left her bedroom with her chin angled determinedly and almost collided with Madame d'Armor. Apologising hastily and rather breathlessly, she wondered just how Paul had explained their sudden decision to go out to dinner, and she eyed the old lady uncertainly for a moment. It was possible she might object to her grandson wining and dining her husband's latest employee, but Jesamine thought not.

"Paul has told me of your plans to drive into Nantes for dinner, *mon enfant*," she told her, but still betrayed nothing of her own feelings in the matter.

Jesamine laughed, a vague uneasy laugh. "They were rather more Paul's plans than mine, *madame*," she told her. "He isn't the easiest person to refuse, as you'll know!"

Clothilde d'Armor studied her flushed face for a moment and Jesamine could not even guess what was going on behind those kindly eyes. Then she placed a hand on her arm and shook her head, frowning slightly. "But did you wish to refuse, *enfant*?" she asked.

Jesamine, not even sure if she knew the answer herself, took a moment or two to answer. Certainly she had no real objection to going with him, except for lack of confidence in her own willpower she would have been delighted with the prospect. "I didn't actually want to refuse," she said. "It's just that – " She shrugged, laughing again, that vague uneasy laugh. "Oh, of course I want to go!" she said with determined conviction. "I'll have a marvellous time and probably get a little drunk to celebrate my first evening out in France – my first for over two months!"

"Jesamine, *ma chère* – " Madame d'Armor's slender fingers tightened suddenly on her arm and there was something in her manner that Jesamine found both puzzling and disturbing. She hesitated to go on as if, having started, she regretted her impulsiveness, and Jesamine waited patiently for her to go on. The look in her eyes suggested anxiety rather than disapproval, so it was not that she objected to the outing. "I have become – fond of you, *mon enfant*," she went on after a while. "I feel for you almost as if you were – my own."

"Louise," Jesamine whispered, and gently squeezed the

fingers on her arm.

During the more than two months that Jesamine had been at the château not one word had been said of Louise d'Armor, and it occurred to her as she looked at the old lady how much of a strain such reticence must impose on her. She must have loved Louise very much; Clothilde d'Armor was the kind of woman who would dote on an only daughter, but it was debatable whether a complete and unending silence on the subject of her life and death was in any way a comfort to her.

"You know?" The dark eyes had a touchingly anxious look that Jesamine found affecting, and again she squeezed her fingers gently.

"Only that she lived for a very short time, *madame*," she told her.

Madame d'Armor was nodding her understanding. "Ah *oui*," she said, "*la chapelle!*"

So Paul had told her about that unauthorised visit to the little chapel – it did not really surprise her. "I found the little church by accident," she explained carefully. It was like breaking down the first staves in a barrier, and she almost held her breath for fear she trod too carelessly and the subject was closed to her again. "Madame d'Armor, if you – "

At that moment she caught sight of Paul striding along the gallery towards them, and withdrew her hand swiftly from the old lady's arm. It would not be beyond Paul to suspect such confidence with his grandmother and she had no desire to raise controversies here and now. She regretted that the moment was lost, for she guessed that it would not be easy to establish another such moment of rapport, but she drew back from letting Paul know that she had been close to hearing about his mother at last. She had seen too often how he reacted to any suggestion of curiosity from her on that subject.

He was not wearing evening dress, but a dark grey suit of impeccable cut that fitted his tall lean frame to perfection. A cream shirt threw his rugged brown features into contrast, and the now familiar smell of his aftershave completely banished any connection with the heat and dust of the vineyards where he spent the greater part of his days. Seeing him so well groomed, so assertively and aggressively masculine, she felt herself trembling despite her vow to keep a firm control on the situation.

She had changed into a pale green dress and draped a soft cream cashmere shawl around her shoulders instead of a wrap, and his grey eyes swept appraisingly over her as he placed an arm lightly about his grandmother's shoulders. Bending his head, he kissed her brow with a gentleness that could still surprise Jesamine.

"You will forgive us, Grand'mère, *n'est-ce pas?*" he begged in that deeply persuasive voice that Jesamine was all too familiar with, and Madame d'Armor turned her head and looked up at him.

"You will be late?" she guessed, and he smiled, that slightly wolfish smile that made Jesamine's pulses flutter warningly.

"*Mais oui, chèrie,* almost certainly we will be late!" Once more he looked at Jesamine and one fair brow was raised enquiringly. "*N'est-ce pas,* Jesamine?" he asked, as if it was she who would ultimately decide what time they returned. "You do not have – scruples that demand you return to the château on the stroke of midnight, like Cendrillon, do you, *ma chère?*"

"No, of course I don't!" She denied it hastily, but flushed under Madame d'Armor's curious scrutiny. She gripped her hands tightly over the small evening purse she carried and fervently hoped that he was not going to start off the evening by trying to make her angry. "And I assure you, Paul," she told him, "that I don't feel in the least like Cinderella!"

For several seconds she looked at him and his eyes glittered with laughter, so that she wondered rather despairingly if it was going to be so different after all. But then he laughed and shook his head, bending once more to kiss his grandmother's forehead. "*Très bien,*" he said, "then let us go, *petite,* before it grows too late! *Au revoir,* Grand'mère, *à tout a l'heure!*"

"Paul!" He turned back to her, his hand already under Jesamine's elbow, ready to go, and the old lady looked at him for a second, then spoke to him in rapid and urgent French, her eyes anxious.

He smiled, a slow warm smile that was reassuring even without words, and he left Jesamine for a moment and took his grandmother's hand in his. He too spoke in his own tongue, his voice low and persuasive, then he raised the old lady's hand to his lips and kissed her fingers. "*Ne te fâche pas, chère,*" he told her, and once more took Jesamine's arm.

It was getting dark as they drove out of Grosvallée and on up the steep road where she had had her first encounter with Paul, and Jesamine wondered if he too remembered the incident. She had been over the spot only the once, and could not be sure she would recognise it again, especially in the near darkness, but Paul turned suddenly and smiled at her as they approached a sharp bend with the valley falling away below.

"What shall we do if a *petite idiote* in a hired *auto* comes around this bend on the wrong side of the road, *ma chère?*" he asked, then laughed as he gave his attention to the road once more.

"Treat her a little more gallantly than you did me, I

hope!" Jesamine retorted swiftly, but found it hard not to smile as she looked at the rugged profile barely discernible in the deepening darkness. It seemed their relationship had been fraught with incident from the beginning, and she wondered if it could ever be any different. "Do you realise," she asked him, "that I've never been this far since?"

"*Non?*" For a moment she glimpsed the white gleam of his smile and guessed his eyes were bright with that familiar and disturbing laughter. "Do you feel that you have been – neglected, *ma chère?*" he asked, and she hastily sought to deny any such implication.

"Oh no, of course not!" she said. "I wasn't complaining, I merely remarked on the fact that I haven't been further than the village since I arrived – I've been too busy!"

"You have worked hard with Grandpère's *trésors*," he said. "It is time that you escaped for a while, *n'est-ce pas?*"

He sounded perfectly serious about it, and she believed he was, but it was rather deflating to think that pity for her lack of social life had been his reason for asking her out. "Is that why you asked me out to dinner?" she asked impulsively, and he laughed shortly, startling her with his reaction.

"*Mais non, petite,*" he denied firmly. "I do not ask pretty girls to dine with me because I feel sorry for them! You flatter me if you think me so soft-hearted!" She said nothing, but felt strangely light-headed as she eased herself more comfortably against the deep leather seat. A few seconds later he turned his head again, looking over his shoulder at her, and she could only guess at the expression in his eyes, for it was too dark to judge now. "You did not believe that I would ask you for such a reason, did you, Jesamine?" he asked, and she turned her head lazily to look at him.

"I wasn't sure," she confessed.

Paul laughed, a short impatient sound, as he handled the

big car round another bend in the road. "You will be *quite* sure before this evening is finished, *ma belle*!" he promised. "But first we will be civilised and have dinner, huh?" He laughed again, but this time more softly, and she found her hands curling tightly over the little purse she carried.

It was not the moment to question his meaning, even had she needed to, so she remained silent. Instead she looked out of the window at the lights that twinkled from houses down in the valley among those endless vineyards, and the river gleaming like pewter in the moonlight as it wound its way to the estuary and the sea. She would need all her will power if she was to remain firm against falling head over heels in love with him – and he was not going to make it easy for her.

It was quite late when they drove into Nantes, but she had grown accustomed to the French habit of dining late and it was more excitement than hunger that stirred her pulses as they drove through the well lit streets. What did concern her to some extent was the possibility of meeting someone he knew, and she particularly had his women friends in mind.

He had never made any secret of his taste for feminine company, and various remarks of his grandfather's had served only to enlarge on a reputation he had hinted at himself. It was not as if she was a child, or even a naïve girl, but she felt as if she was being torn in two directions at once. She could not forget the delirious excitement of being in his arms earlier that same evening, for it had been like nothing she had ever known before and her senses still tingled when she thought about it. At the same time common sense told her that if she was to keep control on the situation she must not let the same circumstances occur again.

To Paul she would be just another affair and, as she

glanced at him from the corners of her eyes, she felt a sudden wild urge to get away from him before she made an utter and complete fool of herself. If only she had gone back with James when he wanted her to, or had let him stay within call – but it was too late now. Too late to wish James was close by, and too late to regret having come out with Paul and, shaking her head over her own folly, she looked again out of the window.

Nantes was built on the estuary of the river Loire and the streets alongside the river itself might have been in another world. Fine old houses that had once been occupied by wealthy merchants overlooked the river and had walled gardens that scented the night air with the scent of roses and carnations.

The great castle, once the home of the Dukes of Brittany, loomed over the whole city and dominated it completely, reminding her that the notorious Gilles de Rais had once lived there too. He was, she recalled, the original Blue-beard, and in her present situation it was an uneasy recollection. The wind was much more fresh this much closer to the sea, and it tickled her bare arms with cool fingers as she walked the short distance to the restaurant with Paul.

There was a bar, straight off the street and quite crowded with people, though Paul got served quickly enough. He handed her a glass of champagne which she took without comment, although such extravagance would have been remarkable at home, and seated himself beside her with his long legs casually crossed one over the other.

"*Ma belle* Jesamine!" he said, and raised his glass to her, his grey eyes bright and challenging.

Hastily avoiding his eyes, she made her own toast a silent one, but sipped her champagne thankfully – she was going to need some Dutch courage before the evening was out, and champagne was as pleasant a way as any to gain it. Her heart was hammering hard at her ribs and she wished she could feel as cool and controlled as she wanted to be.

"You are very quiet, *ma chère*," he said, looking at her steadily over the rim of his glass. "What is troubling you?"

Jesamine shook her head, but it was plain he did not believe her, and after a second or so he reached out and lightly touched her bare arm with his forefinger, stroking it slowly downwards in a shivering caress that brought a new urgency to her heartbeat. "There's nothing troubling me," she told him. "Why should there be, Paul?"

The grey eyes searched her face, slightly narrowed but with an unexpected gentleness in their depths as he placed his hand over her arm, the strong fingers pressing into her soft skin. "You are not a child, I know that well enough, *chérie*," he said, too quietly for anyone sitting close by to hear, "but sometimes I feel that you regard me with the suspicion of a child who does not understand what is going on."

How she was expected to react, Jesamine had no idea, but her instinctive reaction was to look at him with the same sombre darkness in her blue eyes that she had seen reflected in her mirror earlier on. "Maybe I am a little suspicious," she allowed, "but if I am it's because –" She shook her head slowly, seeking the right words. "I know your reputation, Paul," she went on in a small husky voice, "both you and your grandfather have left me in little doubt about it, but I'm not prepared to – to join the ranks as one of your – casual affairs. I'm sorry," she added, hastily and breathlessly, when he did not reply, "but I had to say it!"

It surprised her that he did not immediately flare into anger as she expected, but instead he merely sat beside her sipping his champagne and his eyes were hidden by lowered lids as he gazed down into his drink. "So, now you have said it," he told her, then looked up suddenly and straight into her eyes, and his own had a curious and unfamiliar expression that she did not recognise. "You will now perhaps tell me, *ma chère*, why it is that you are here with me when you feel so strongly about – joining the ranks?"

"Paul, I didn't – "

A long finger placed firmly over her lips silenced her, and he was shaking his head. "I do not wish to hear, after all," he told her, and laughed shortly before tossing off the last of his champagne. "I do not like to have my appetite spoiled before an excellent meal. Come, *chérie*, at least pretend that you like me enough to eat dinner with me, hmm?"

He slid off the bar stool and put a hand under her arm, his fingers gripping tightly, and Jesamine tried not to let a sudden and inexplicable tearfulness become embarrassingly obvious. If only he knew how wrong he was, but – She stopped short suddenly and stared, so that Paul looked down at her curiously.

"Jesamine?"

She licked her lips as he turned and followed her gaze, and in that moment James spotted her and came hurrying through the crowded bar towards them, his perennially boyish features beaming a smile, and with eyes only for her. Glancing hastily at her companion, she saw his brows contract into a frown. "It seems Monsieur Terril grows tired of waiting for you to return, and has come to find you," Paul observed in a flat cool voice, and the hand under her arm tightened its hold imperceptibly as James joined them.

"Jess!" He bent and kissed her with a boisterousness that was both unexpected and embarrassing, then he held her at arms' length and looked at her critically, still ignoring Paul. "You look great," he told her. "Prettier than ever and – blooming!"

Jesamine's smile was a little tight and uncertain. She was not sure whether she welcomed James' sudden appearance or not, even after her earlier regrets, and when she glanced again at Paul it was evident that he resented the intrusion. "James," she said, her gaze unconsciously appealing as she looked at Paul, "you remember Monsieur Paul d'Armor, of course?"

James extended a hand. "Monsieur d'Armor!" The greeting was as short as it politely could be, and Paul for his part merely inclined his head in the briefest of bows. "You're dining here?" James asked, and Jesamine hesitated, wondering if it had to be inevitable that James joined them for dinner.

Paul, however, already had the matter in hand. "Unfortunately, Monsieur Terril," he said, "we cannot ask you to join us. Our table is for two only, you understand, and the popularity of this restaurant – " He shrugged, ostensibly with regret. "It is not possible to make room for an extra one!"

James knew when he was being rebuffed and his normally friendly blue eyes had an icy glitter of dislike as he nodded his head. "Oh, sure," he said, "I understand! But you'll come and have a drink with me, won't you? I'm so – stunned at seeing you here, Jess, I *need* a drink!"

"Paul?"

She looked up into that implacable face and knew he was going to refuse, even before he spoke. Her heart was thudding hard at her ribs while the grey eyes held hers for a moment and she could not even guess what was going on behind them. But he was shaking his head firmly.

"Our regrets, *monsieur*," he said, coolly polite, "but we have dinner waiting for us." He would have turned away with that, and taken Jesamine with him, but James was not quite so easily deterred.

"Hey now, wait a minute," he insisted, "I'd like a couple of words with Jess! I was going to call you in the morning, love," he told her. "I'd like to take a look around while I'm here this time, and I'd like you to come with me." He looked at Paul, narrow-eyed and challenging. "Is it O.K. if I pick you up about ten in the morning?"

"About ten?" She was aware of the pressure of those hard strong fingers on her arm, and she licked her lips anxiously as she glanced up once more from the corner of her eye.

"I presume your boss won't object," James said, looking directly at Paul, and Jesamine shook her head.

"I'm sure Monsieur d'Armor won't mind," she assured him. "Paul isn't my boss," she added, catching his look, "his grandfather is, and he's a kindly man – he'll understand."

"Good!" James nodded. "Then I presume he won't mind if I pick you up from the château – O.K.?"

"Oh, yes." She was not sure what Monsieur d'Armor would say to James collecting her for a day's outing, but she thought he would not mind too much.

"Fine!" He took her hand in his, a small and rather rueful smile on his mobile mouth. "And you're sure you won't have that drink?" he asked.

"*Non, merci, monsieur!*" Paul's firm voice answered for them both, and the hand under her arm urged her to hurry. There was simply no point in trying to resist, even had she wanted to. "You will excuse us," he said. "*Bonsoir*, Monsieur Terril – perhaps we will meet again!"

"More than likely," James agreed, "if I'm coming to pick up Jess in the morning! Oh, incidentally," he added, as if the thought had only now come to mind, "I was talking to a man the other day who was at the Sorbonne before the war, he said he knew a girl there called d'Armor – would that have been any relation of yours, do you think?"

For several seconds Paul said nothing, nor did he move, but he looked at James with narrowed eyes that glittered like ice in that tanned, rugged face, and Jesamine shivered. It was as if someone had run an icy finger down her spine, and she held her breath while she waited for Paul to reply to what she was certain James had intended as a dig at the man he disliked so much.

"It is possible, Monsieur Terril," he said coolly at last. "By tradition our family are educated at the University of Paris – I was myself."

"And your – mother too?" James insisted relentlessly, while Jesamine curled her hands tightly, her heart thudding anxiously at her ribs.

She knew James did not like Paul, mostly because he did not trust him in proximity to herself, but she was appalled to think that he could raise a subject as delicate as this in such a public place, and at such a time. She looked at him reproachfully, but he carefully avoided her eyes and she guessed he was already regretting his impulsive malice.

"My mother was also at the Sorbonne, *monsieur*," Paul agreed with a coolness that surprised Jesamine. "And now, if you will excuse us – we would like to have dinner. *Bonne nuit, monsieur!*"

Firmly holding her arm, he steered her in the direction of the restaurant, and she looked up at him, wondering how on earth she could convince him that she had not once suggested to James that he find out what he could about Louise d'Armor. She licked her lips anxiously as they made their way through the crowd and sought words to counteract the heavy silence that was between them.

"Paul." He looked down at her, and she took courage from the fact that there was more curiosity than anger in his eyes. "I – I knew nothing about that," she told him in a slightly breathless voice. "I'd no idea James would – come out with anything so – " She drew a deep unsteady breath. "I know how you resent anyone asking about your moth –

your family, and I wouldn't have dreamed of asking James to find out anything, I mean I wouldn't – "

"I know, *ma chère*." His quietness surprised her, and his smile even more. "I resent questions about my family simply because I do not consider our private affairs any concern of any but ourselves," he told her. "There is nothing sinister in our reticence, merely a desire for privacy – something to which we are entitled, I think you will agree."

"Yes, of course!"

The grey eyes looked down at her steadily, and the wide mouth hinted at a smile. "Then let us not speak of it again, *petite*, hmm?" he suggested.

In the doorway of the restaurant she could see across to the bar, and she could see James still standing there, having that drink Paul had so resolutely refused to share with him. And she wondered why James had seen fit to so nearly ruin her evening – although at the back of her mind, she thought she knew.

With a morsel of *crêpe suzette* on her fork and balanced midway between her plate and her mouth, Jesamine looked up and caught Paul's eye on her. There was a flutter of sensation in the region of her heart as she hastily put the pancake into her mouth, then looked across at him again as she swallowed it and reached for her wine glass.

"He does not like me, your James," he said calmly, and so unexpectedly that Jesamine stared at him without answering. "It is understandable, *naturellement*," he added without waiting for her to comment. "He is jealous because you are with me and not with him, where he thinks you should be!"

Jesamine shook her head. She had long since put James and his unexpected lack of tact to the back of her mind, and instead given all her attention to her companion and her dinner in that order. Now the subject had been abruptly brought to light again and she was not at all sure that she liked it. She had expected Paul to let it lapse gratefully, in view of his usual reticence on the subject of his family, but she thought James himself was foremost in his mind at the moment, not his unfortunate *gaffe*.

She carefully put down her fork but did not look at him, instead she toyed with the stem of her empty wine glass. "I wish you wouldn't – you and your grandfather – keep labouring under the delusion that James is – in love with me," she said, her voice curiously husky. "He isn't, I know he isn't."

"You lack perception if you think so," Paul told her confidently. "Though I do not believe that you return his love, *ma chère*, and perhaps that is why you remain so – blind to his feelings."

"I like James," she said, twirling the glass between her fingers and watching it shine in the light rather than look at him as she spoke. "I like him a great deal, but I don't love him, and I – I *hope* he doesn't love me. I wouldn't like to hurt him." She put down her glass and rested her elbows on the table in front of her, looking at him at last simply because she wanted to impress him with what she was saying. "Now can we please not talk about James?" she said.

He held her gaze steadily for several seconds, his own grey eyes narrowed thoughtfully, then he smiled, a wry, lop-sided smile that pulled at one corner of his mouth. "I do not believe you welcomed his sudden appearance," he said, as it if was something he wanted to be true, and Jesamine shook her head.

"I don't know whether I did or not," she confessed.

For a moment he was silent, then he shook his head and a trace of that smile still remained. "*Très bien, ma chère,*" he said, "we will not talk of James again."

Several glasses of champagne had induced a mood that was less suspicious of anything he said than she usually was, and when she saw his eyes watching her some time later, she smiled, her own susceptible emotions responding to him.

"Why are you looking at me like that?" she asked, and Paul laughed, shaking his head slowly.

"How do I look at you, *ma chère*?" he countered.

"I don't know, sort of – " She shrugged, a little flutter of sensation curling in her stomach as she sought refuge in twirling the champagne glass in her fingers again. Her hands felt strangely unsteady as she held the slender stem, and she knew her cheeks were flushed with warm colour. "I think I've had too much champagne," she said with an unsteady little laugh, and covered her glass with one hand when he picked up the bottle again. "No," she said. "No more, Paul, please!"

His eyes travelled slowly over her face and came to rest on the tremulous softness of her mouth, then he shook his head and refilled his own glass. "Are you so afraid of becoming *insensible, petite*?" he teased, and his accent, she noticed a little hazily, was becoming more pronounced.

Combined with that deep, soft voice it was *séduisant,* she thought, recalling her limited French, then brought herself hastily back to earth as she avoided his gaze. "I don't intend getting drunk," she informed him. "I'm not used to so much champagne – we're not brought up on it, you know, like French children are!"

"*Champagne?*" The deep glow in his eyes warmed her whole body as she listened to him, and he laughed. "French children are for the most part brought up on *vin ordinaire, ma chérie,*" he told her with a smile. "Not many of them are born with a taste for champagne!"

"Unless of course they happen to be wealthy little boys

with the name of d'Armor," she guessed rashly, and his eyes held hers for several seconds before he shook his head.

"Does it – offend you so much, my being wealthy?" he asked.

"Offend – " She stared at him. "No, of course it doesn't offend me," she said a little breathlessly. "Why on earth should it?"

He said nothing for a moment, but continued to hold her with that steady and rather disconcerting gaze. Then he shrugged. "*Je ne sais pas, petite*," he said. "How would I know? You do not always need a reason, do you?"

"Paul – " She hesitated, looking at him for a second or two before she shrugged uneasily and shook her head. "No," she said firmly, "I refuse to spoil the rest of this lovely evening by starting even a mild argument with you!" She laughed a little unsteadily. "I really think I must have had far too much champagne," she said. "I feel very light-headed, and I know I must look slightly tipsy – "

Paul took her hand in his and briefly his mouth was pressed to the soft warmth of her palm. "*Alléchante!*" he murmured, his lips brushing her palm in a flutter of sensation that made her shiver.

Vaguely at the back of her mind was the thought that she ought to do something about such a blatant display in a place as public as a crowded restaurant, but somehow she could not seem to find either the words or the inclination to object. Instead she looked at the top of the fair head as it bowed over her hand and felt a curious sense of occasion. Her whole body was aglow and her lips were parted in breathless anticipation as she reached out with her free hand and touched his face; lightly, almost fearfully, beside the strong jaw.

"Paul!"

He looked up and his eyes still had that deep glowing

warmth in them. Covering the hand that was touching his face he pressed it to the firm tanned flesh with his own strong fingers. "Shall we go, *chérie*?" he asked in a voice that was little more than a whisper, and Jesamine did not answer at once. "I want you to myself!"

Her heart was hammering hard at her ribs, beating like a wild thing that sought to escape, and she felt as if they were suddenly alone. It was the moment she had both longed for and dreaded; the moment when she must decide whether she was prepared to belong to him for a time, no matter how short, or whether to be firm, now, before her emotions became too involved for there to *be* any choice.

Her voice was shiveringly unsteady, but she had made her choice and she must make it clear to him now, before it was too late. She could not face losing him again if she once had his love, she had not the strength to go out of his life, not the way Louise Sutton had out of Charles Louis Vernais's. Drawing her hand from his clasp as gently as possible, she folded both her hands together in front of her, trying to stop their trembling.

"Paul," she said, barely audible in the hubbub of the restaurant, "I can't – you know I can't just – "

"I ask that you come with me, *ma chérie*," he urged. "That you listen to me for just a little while, hmm?" His voice was deep, quiet, *séduisant*, just as Charles Louis's had probably been, and she shivered at the sound of it, but she was still shaking her head determinedly, and Paul's mouth tightened. "You refuse even to listen to what I have to say?" he demanded harshly, and she looked up at him, her eyes dark and anxious. It was such a sudden and unhappy way to end a lovely evening, and she regretted it more than he could ever realise.

"I – think I know what you have to say," she whispered. "But I – " She shook her head, troubled because words usually came easily to her. "You know what I'm trying to say, Paul," she said, "I tried to tell you earlier on this evening. I – I can't let myself become any more deeply involved with you, not when I know it won't – it can't last!"

"One man, one woman – every woman's ideal!" He repeated the phrase cynically, and she flinched as if he had struck her. Filling his glass from the almost empty champagne bottle, he raised it in mock salute before emptying it in one draught. "Why is it so hard for you to – *Zut*!" He swore impatiently and looked at her as if he tried hard to understand her and failed. "Why are you so afraid of love, *mon petit ange*?" he asked.

Meeting his eyes, she felt her own mist over and despaired of making her sudden weakness so obvious. "Why do you find it so hard to love?" she countered in a small, husky voice. "Why does it always have to be an – *affaire de coeur*, Paul? Why never the real thing?"

He put down his glass slowly and he no longer looked at her, then he called over the waiter and settled the bill, all without an unnecessary word, and finally he helped her to her feet with a hand under her arm, and she shrank from the coldness of him as they made their way through the crowded restaurant again.

Outside in the warm night air she took a moment to breathe in the freshness after the close atmosphere of the restaurant, then she looked up at him, not quite sure what she wanted to say, but appalled by the barrier between them. "Paul – " She tried to see his face more clearly, but there were tears in earnest now, rolling down her cheeks and filling her eyes, and there seemed nothing she could do about it.

He did not turn his head nor look down at her, but kept his hand under her elbow as they walked along the shadowed street. "You need have no fear, *enfant*," he told her in a flat cool voice, "I will return you at once to the safe keeping of my *grand'mère*! You are in no danger from me!"

Jesamine said nothing, but sat beside him in the car as they drove back along the Grosvallée road, crying silently in the darkness and wishing James had not come back. For with him came the temptation to go back home and try to forget about Paul d'Armor – even though she knew it was already too late for that.

CHAPTER TEN

JESAMINE was unable to face the prospect of breakfast the following morning, knowing that both Monsieur and Madame d'Armor would be curious about their unexpectedly early return the night before. Neither could she face Paul across the breakfast table with any degree of self-confidence, so she sent her apologies via the maid and took more than her customary time over getting up.

They would still be at breakfast, she thought, as she came downstairs, and she hesitated for a moment when the *salon* door opened. It was not Paul, however, but Brigitte, and the housekeeper looked up and smiled when she saw her, waiting for her to come down into the hall. "Monsieur Terril has telephoned, *mademoiselle*," she told her. "I am to make the apology, but he cannot now see you as he had planned. He will telephone you at some other time today."

"Oh!" Jesamine looked stunned for a moment. "Thank you, Brigitte."

"You are ill, *mademoiselle*?" Brigitte's plain but kindly face expressed concern, and Jesamine smiled.

"Oh no, Brigitte, thank you," she told her. "I'm all right."

"*Très bien, mademoiselle!*" The housekeeper left her, but she was still concerned, it was obvious, and Jesamine made her way to the library, feeling almost as tearful as she had last night.

She picked up the list she had been working on for the past few days, but her mind was not on what she was doing, instead she kept seeing Paul's face as it had been last night — firm and unrelenting. She shook her head, impatient with her own weakness, and walked over to stand in the window, gazing out at the gardens, mellow and full-blown in the August sun.

The door behind her opened and she swung round quickly, her eyes wide and anxious and a wild turbulent beating in her heart, for she knew who it would be as surely as she knew that Brigitte had told him where she was. In dark slacks and a navy shirt he had a sombre look that contrasted with his more usual appearance, but her senses still responded to him as urgently and she shook back her hair in a gesture that betrayed her nervousness.

He stood just inside the door, looking across at her, and his voice had that deep, soft tone that was always so affecting, though never more so than now. "Jesamine?" he said, moving across the room to her. "Are you all right?"

The question confirmed Brigitte's part in his being there and she nodded, not quite meeting those grey eyes that looked at her so disturbingly. "I'm all right," she said huskily. "Just a little apprehensive, that's all. James rang to say he isn't coming for me this morning."

He frowned, plainly curious. "And that makes you apprehensive?"

Jesamine lifted her shoulders. It was not quite a shrug, but it defined the uncertainty she felt. "Only because I hope he isn't – " She hesitated, seeking suitable words to say what she had to say without arousing his antagonism. "He mentioned something about someone at the University of – "

"My mother," Paul said quietly, and she stared at him for a moment in stunned surprise. He looked at her steadily, as if making up his mind, then, briefly, a hint of smile touched his mouth and he took another step towards her, bringing him within touching distance and setting her pulses racing again. "You knew it was Louise d'Armor he referred to, did you not, *ma chère*?" he asked quietly.

She found it incredibly hard to answer with the grey eyes fixed on her so steadily. All the weeks she had known him and his family, never once had Louise d'Armor been mentioned; he had even threatened to send her packing if she asked questions in the village. Something had happened since last night, something she could not even guess at, but which had brought him, quiet and confiding, to find her this morning.

"I – guessed," she admitted. "It wasn't difficult, although I've never discussed it with James, I swear it, Paul. He must have – "

"He was consumed with the same curiosity as you were, *ma petite*," Paul teased her gently.

"A curiosity you despised me for," she suggested in a small husky voice, and he shook his head in immediate denial.

"Not despised you, Jesamine, but I was not – ready to tell you then."

"And now?" she prompted.

He studied her face for several seconds in silence, then shook his head slowly. "Last night," he said in that deep, soft voice, "I lay in the darkness of my room for many hours and thought of you, this morning, with James Terril. I was resolved this morning to have no secrets from you, to tell you as much of Louise d'Armor as I know myself. Will you hear me, *chèrie*?"

The tears that had for so long been held back stood bright and glistening in her eyes as she looked at him, and she wanted more than ever to reach out and touch him. "You know I will," she said.

He spoke of Louise d'Armor, she realised as he began the story of his mother's tragically short life, as if she was a stranger, someone he had only heard of but never met, and it took her several minutes to realise that that was exactly what Louise was to him. Merely a name in the past, a stranger he had never met.

"She was a student at the University of Paris, as Monsieur Terril said," he told her, "and so, also, was my father, Paul Müller. They were parted when war became imminent and he went back to Germany. Then, by one of those coincidences that make life so – unbelievable at times, he was sent with the occupation forces to this area and, *naturellement*, they met again."

"On opposite sides," Jesamine whispered, and he nodded agreement.

"It was not the easiest of situations," he said. "Nothing had changed as far as they were concerned and, after a while, they began to meet again secretly. It was not possible any other way, for my family have never been collaborators. It must have taken much pleading from Louise, but eventually, in the strictest secrecy, Père Dominic in his capacity as chaplain to the d'Armors married them in the family chapel, with Monsieur Marais, a close friend who could be trusted, as a witness."

"The schoolteacher!"

"*Mais oui*," Paul agreed with a slight twitch of his wide mouth. "You also have met with him, I think, via his son!" He gave her no time to reply but went on with his narrative, still in that strangely impersonal voice. "It was impossible for the ceremony to be made public knowledge, *naturellement*, but it was inevitable that at some time someone was sure to see them together, and by then Louise was heavy with child."

"That fact may have saved her from the attentions of the local resistance group, they may have thought her an unwilling victim, or it might have been that the d'Armor family were still in good standing with the people of Grosvallée. Whatever the reason, Paul Müller was found mysteriously drowned in the river one morning. It was assumed by his superiors that he had slipped and fallen while crossing the bridge, so there were no reprisals taken, but that same morning Brigitte found Louise dazed and wandering in the grounds of the château. She was delivered of her child, and died within hours."

Jesamine shivered, wondering for a second how he could seem so untouched by it, and perhaps, only days ago, she might have gone on believing he was unaffected. Only now she thought she knew him better, and saw beyond the impersonal tone of his voice and the steely coolness of his eyes, reaching out to the man behind them.

"Paul." She whispered his name, no more, and he looked at her and smiled, as if it was a relief to talk of it at last.

"Père Dominic's part in the affair had to be concealed, *naturellement*," he said. "He was a brave man, but he would have been in trouble with both sides if it had been discovered that he had performed a marriage ceremony. No one but Père Dominic and Pierre Marais know that I am other than – " His broad shoulders shrugged off the inevitable burden he had had to bear for all his thirty-odd years. "I am known as Paul d'Armor, and I have no fault to find with the name I bear."

"Why should you?" Jesamine asked quietly. She looked up at him for a second, then shook her head. "I – I wanted so much to say I was sorry last night," she went on. "I shouldn't have said the things I did to you about – about falling in love. No matter if you were – unkind," she hurried on breathlessly when he would have spoken, "I shouldn't have been quite so – personal." She tried to laugh, but it was no more than an odd little sound more reminiscent of a sob, and she went on again hastily. "I had far too much champagne," she said, "that will have to be my excuse!"

"And what will be *my* excuse, *petite*?" Paul asked softly. He took the one more step that brought their bodies into contact. A light, nebulous touch that made her shiver and brought a swift urgency to her pulse. He took the list from her then enclosed her hands in his own, his strong fingers moving over hers with infinite gentleness. "I hurt you," he said, and shook his head, as if he expected her to deny it. "I think I meant to hurt you, *chérie*, because I was afraid to admit what you could – what you had already done to me."

Jesamine raised her eyes, every nerve crying out for him to hold her in his arms. She could not yet believe what was happening, but she wanted so much to believe that she half-closed her eyes as she looked up at him, and swayed a little closer. "What *have* I done to you?" she whispered, and his arms slid around her, pressing her so close that she could feel the urgent pressure of his body as if it was part of her own.

"One man, one woman," he reminded her in a soft voice. "I have lain for long hours in the night learning your creed, *ma chérie*, but I want it to be so with us, if you will let it." He bent his head and pressed his mouth to the softness of her neck, his voice muffled by her long hair. "*Je t'aime, ma petite* – I love you!"

Jesamine looked up at him with eyes that were dark with the tumult of emotions that swept through her like fire, urging her to think of nothing beyond the fact that he loved her. She lifted her arms and put them around his neck, searching that strong rugged face for a moment as if she could still not quite believe it.

"I was – afraid," she confessed in a voice that still shivered with uncertainty. "I loved you and I was afraid you – "

"Last night when I lay thinking of you into the small hours," Paul said, his mouth against hers, "I thought of you meeting with James Terril this morning, and I knew you were not one to be taken lightly and forgotten, *mon amour*. When Brigitte came to tell me that you were here – alone, I came to find you, *ma chère petite*, to confess how I felt." He kissed her mouth lightly, barely touching her lips with his. "Will you marry me, *mon amour*?" he whispered.

"Oh, Paul!" She looked at him with bright glistening eyes that gave him his answer without words. "*Je t'aime, mon chéri!*"

Paul laughed, shaking his head over her accent, but drawing her closer still as he sought her mouth. Her lips parted and she yielded willingly to the urgent hunger of his kiss, pressing close to him, sure at last that he was as unshakably in love as she was herself. It was quite a lot later that she thought about Louise Sutton. Louise and Charles Louis Vernais had started it all, and now, two hundred years later, there was to be a happy ending at last – it was as she had always visualised it.

the omnibus

A Great Idea! Three great romances by the same author, in one deluxe paperback volume.

A Great Value! Almost 600 pages of pure entertainment for only $1.95 a volume.

Listed below are the Omnibus volumes that have recently been available at your favorite bookstore.

Essie Summers #1
Bride in Flight (#933)
Meet on My Ground (#1326)
Postscript to Yesterday (#1119)

Jean S. MacLeod
The Wolf of Heimra (#990)
Summer Island (#1314)
Slave of the Wind (#1339)

Eleanor Farnes
The Red Cliffs (#1335)
The Flight of the Swan (#1280)
Sister of the Housemaster (#975)

Sara Seale
Queen of Hearts (#1324)
Penny Plain (#1197)
Green Girl (#1045)

Violet Winspear #1
Palace of the Peacocks (#1318)
Beloved Tyrant (#1032)
Court of the Veils (#1267)

Isobel Chace
A Handful of Silver (#1306)
The Saffron Sky (#1250)
The Damask Rose (#1334)

Due to popular demand for these great volumes, most titles have been complete sellouts. If you missed any of these Omnibus volumes or want additional information on more than 30 other volumes, please fill in and send us the coupon on the next page.

Harlequin Omnibus

SEND TO: → **Harlequin Reader Service,**
M.P.O. Box 707,
Niagara Falls, N.Y. 14302

CANADIAN RESIDENTS → **Harlequin Reader Service,**
Stratford, Ont. N5A 6W4

Please check volumes requested:

☐ Essie Summers #1   ☐ Sara Seale
☐ Jean S. MacLeod   ☐ Violet Winspear #1
☐ Eleanor Farnes   ☐ Isobel Chace

Please send me by return mail the books that I have checked.
I am enclosing $1.95 for each book ordered.

Number of books ordered _____ @ $1.95 each = $_____

Postage and Handling = _____.25

TOTAL $_____

☐ Please send me by return mail additional information on the
Harlequin Omnibus.

Name_____

Address_____

City_____

State/Prov._____

Zip/Postal Code_____

BY POPULAR DEMAND . . .

36 original novels from this series — by 3 of the world's greatest romance authors.

These back issues by Anne Hampson, Anne Mather, and Violet Winspear have been out of print for some time. So don't miss out, order your copies now!

All the above titles are available at 95¢ each. Please use the attached order form to indicate your requirements.

Offer expires March 31, 1977.

Harlequin Reader Service

ORDER FORM

MAIL COUPON TO ➡

Harlequin Reader Service,
M.P.O. Box 707,
Niagara Falls, New York 14302.

Canadian **SEND**
Residents **TO:** ➡

Harlequin Reader Service,
Stratford, Ont. N5A 6W4

Harlequin Presents...

Please check Volumes requested:

☐ 1   ☐ 2   ☐ 3   ☐ 4   ☐ 5
☐ 7   ☐ 8   ☐ 9   ☐ 10   ☐ 11
☐ 12   ☐ 13   ☐ 14   ☐ 15   ☐ 16
☐ 17   ☐ 18   ☐ 19   ☐ 20   ☐ 21
☐ 22   ☐ 23   ☐ 24   ☐ 25   ☐ 26
☐ 27   ☐ 28   ☐ 29   ☐ 30   ☐ 31
☐ 32   ☐ 33   ☐ 34   ☐ 35   ☐ 36
☐ 37

Please send me by return mail the books which I have checked.
I am enclosing 95¢ for each book ordered.

Number of books ordered _____ @ 95¢ each = $ _____

Postage and Handling = _____ .25

TOTAL = $ _____

Name _____

Address _____

City _____

State/Prov. _____

Zip/Postal Code _____

ROM2018